T0124201

Without LOVE

A Neanderthal's Journey

LDouble JC

authorHOUSE®

AuthorHouse™
1663 Liberty Drive
Bloomington, IN 47403
www.authorhouse.com
Phone: 1 (800) 839-8640

© 2016 LDouble JC. All rights reserved.

Editors:
Erica Casilda Kathleen Zamudio-Ahl
Nicole Black
LDouble JC

Artistry by
Neanderchild
LDouble JC

No part of this book may be reproduced, stored in a retrieval system, or transmitted by any means without the written permission of the author.

Published by AuthorHouse 05/16/2016

ISBN: 978-1-5246-0647-3 (sc)
ISBN: 978-1-5246-0645-9 (hc)
ISBN: 978-1-5246-0646-6 (e)

Library of Congress Control Number: 2016907297

Print information available on the last page.

Any people depicted in stock imagery provided by Thinkstock are models, and such images are being used for illustrative purposes only. Certain stock imagery © Thinkstock.

This book is printed on acid-free paper.

Because of the dynamic nature of the Internet, any web addresses or links contained in this book may have changed since publication and may no longer be valid. The views expressed in this work are solely those of the author and do not necessarily reflect the views of the publisher, and the publisher hereby disclaims any responsibility for them.

Contents

Special thanks to Ashley Budnick,

my two moms, friends,

The Neanderthal, The Mind Shaper, and ice-cream

Preface--To The Reader.

Hello and welcome, thank you for picking up this book. This is an experimental piece of nothing more than a confused, semi-educated Neanderthal Man and a female Mind Shaper trying to figure out life and a certain meaning within oneself. There are some factual pieces of information mixed in with a side of opinion among the pages; either way there is some real knowledge and experience thrown into the mix. We both came to the conclusion that as humans we tend to read what we want, when we want and even sometimes record items down with pen and paper. The items we seek out within creativity is what lies in our own passions through classic books, mathematical equations or just simple items in our own heads that we feel we must get out in an attempt to put down on paper for others to enjoy. That is what this is, and nothing more, so please accept this book as an opinion with hints and elements of knowledge, some good information and a couple short stories. If at any time you think you have seen some of the same things in other books, you're probably right; but the fun part about this is that most of what is written between these pages is a commonality of surroundings that we inherent or learn without ever knowing why.

The characters in these pages may be real or made up. The Neanderthal, our main character, is trying to understand the feelings or the emotions associated and depicted through the heart and brain of something so simple and complicated at the same time. On the other side of this creative piece is the Mind Shaper, the Neanderthals counterpart. She's here to keep some slight objectiveness to the Neanderthal allowing for some female perspective as well. Actually, now that we think of it, the thought of a female being a mind shaper is rather clever.

Mind Shaper: "Good job Neanderthal!"

Neanderthal: "No problem, it's what I do!"

When we started conversing about this piece, it didn't seem right to us that this book could be written solely by a man or solely by a woman. We understood that it needed a duel perspective, whether it be through arguments or different communications. The Neanderthal, being single and open to all possibilities and endearments of the world; and opposite The Mind Shaper who has continued on following a more traditional experience is what you the reader will get when relating to the writing between the pages.

We came to the conclusion that there seems to be someone else asking the questions, and the answers and thoughts are not being shared with the world. Are they scared? Would anyone else care? Does it matter to society? Should they read this or not? This book will answer none of that; in fact it is just an idea of the two of us dissecting something that we feel has been abused and misrepresented for too long and nothing more. It will hold a few facts, some individual accounts and maybe even have you as the reader question your own nuances on the subject within. Keep in mind both of us will be inputting thoughts and sections into the writing, from our lives, situations, and experiences. In fact, we think it is essential that both sexes may learn to try to understand some partial mysteries of what the opposite sex may be encompassing when it comes to a certain word that we will dissect, appreciate and more importantly learn to use in different ways.

Guys go ahead and read the girly chapters and sections; you're still not going to understand women any more. But it is important for you know what your girl is possibly thinking, and maybe what she expects from you. Ladies you may get all squishy and emotional, and that's ok. That doesn't mean your guy is any less of a man if he chooses not to read this. But maybe you will gain some slight intuition as to what has propelled men to where they are, and where their understanding resides.

No matter the reason for choosing this book, Thank You. As the reader please do not get all puffed about generalized roles, whether through a traditional or non-traditional stance; we will try to blur and straighten the lines when we can. Now, open your mind and prepare yourself to have the Mind Shaper and the Neanderthal try to explain and disembowel one word. This one word in all of its greatness and dysfunctional nature creates such a powerful stance, but can mean so little at the same time. There is no other word that holds as much power or equality as the one we are about to embark upon. Here is the Modern Day Neanderthal, presenting himself as he learns of this word and how to use it.

p.s. The money you spent to get this piece is helping pay off student loans

Thanks again!

Symbol Enchantment

....pieces for the Neanderthal

"Uug moo ba cha, snu eeerrr click qliuk nnnn mmmmurrrgg thump oooo pth pth uug moo ba;" says the Neanderthal to the female at the first sunset that they share before he thumps her on the head and drags her back to the cave or rock to make her his own. Maybe in these weird grunts is a word that has some of the same meanings or emotions that we or homo-sapiens have had our whole lives and never really knew where it came from or how it came to be.

The world as we know it began (you the reader can decide how; i.e. The Big Bang Theory, God's creation, a magical appearance, or whatever your imagination can come up with) and every living being let it be animal, human, microbial, or spirit holds the instincts of not becoming extinct. The grunts and the moans are what we believe to be part of some type of language over 250,000 years ago to our image of what the first Neanderthal born sounded like. The male, in our minds, would have been strong browed, almost beastly, with a hairy posterior and yielded a club or stick of sorts; possibly poking at a new member of the clan, or outsider, which may be a potential mate. A protector and huntsman type, but extremely wild is what we have come to understand since they had small brains. Though the female may have been an enraged, but submissive being, they too were very animalistic; and it was the instincts of survival to attach themselves to the strongest, or most dominant male figure, to extend life and to go without being hungry or lonely.

We would like to assume they want to feel a bond stronger than a club to the head in hopes of family and survival. These two beings eventually figure out the awkwardness of themselves, choose to mate, and possibly have what we know today as emotions, or at least some feelings upon each other. After the mating ritual, the female starts to change as she holds a bundle within her belly that soon will be the male's new path of teaching or even the new blood line; depending on whether she carries a boy or girl to term, and they are able to grow up. One might be the male's pride, then successor; the other may become his new bride when upon the right age, keeping the clan growing until another male is born. The new being of the two mates cries, spits, shits, and maybe even makes grunts to which the new elements together try to figure out how to survive, all while growing as a family. The male learns how to protect more than himself and the clan; and the female learns to protect her bundle of joy, snarling at anyone who comes near to harm this first identity of family, including the brutality of her mate. This is just a representation to where this one ideal in our world could have come from. Maybe these formed clans were the first representation of humanoids to experience feelings of endearments.

The original Neanderthal may have paved the way to what happens to us the very moment we are born. Even though our modern day medicine and science exists, it is still difficult to figure out the long chain of neurons and wirings still not completely known to man, our brains. As time has changed, our brains have developed to be more complex from that of our original Neanderthal ancestors. Our brains develop and we are pre-destined or are created with some form of pre-notion that allows us to have feelings, emotions, and understandings of life, and our surroundings. We learn how to act, react, or even comprehend and there are many things we encompass; but there is just one intrinsic word that gets implemented or engrained into our everyday lives. It has more meaning and purpose than any other word or feeling, whether shown or stated. It is a four letter word or in our language, but it may have been a mumble, a grunt, or maybe just a certain touch to the original Neanderthals. This is a word that holds a lot of underlying meanings and represents a gamut of emotions, as well as feelings, all the way through our lives; from conception, to our mother having carried us to term, then being raised to adulthood and finally in death as our eulogies are given. Even those whom are abandoned know the word meaning (or lack thereof), but they may not know it fully until they have experienced this word in one of its varying degrees. Just think about how you feel when you do or do not experience the emotional ties that happen with the representations of amore. This book is not about to overuse that very word, in fact, just the opposite. It is a chance to explore its many connotations and feelings through different eyes; maybe the eyes of a Neanderthal and perhaps experience other words to use as an equal or which have the same relevance.

If you're still reading then I welcome you the reader, as the modern day homo sapiens to The Modern Day Neanderthal. You, I, and the rest of the human race are all a bit crazy when it comes to matters of the heart. We tend to throw this word around with heavy difficulty but at the same time with the slightest of ease. Until we let go and explore the possibilities that this one word may mean more than just something to say to others. At the erectus level, you can be judgmental about the Neanderthal because you already know how to start expressing yourself and have the insights and education to what is and is not important when learning the matters of the heart. Though as a homo sapien, would you be able to teach a modern day Neanderthal what this word is without overusing it or abusing what it should represent? The Neanderthal, though, struggles to understand this one crazy, mind altering, passionate word. It has so many passages through life from the past to the present, and is expressed every single day by millions. It makes us wonder if our Neanderthal ancestors actually got to experience these emotions and feelings that go along with the word, or did it just evolve into what it is today? Was it even a word that had meaning, or just something over used and underappreciated, as it seems today? This one word can change the mood of a person instantaneously, but could also be as thrown away as the garbage we create by the pound daily; just leaving all emotions and feelings out the window.

Upon the experiences of the word through many facets of life, it becomes clear that there is no deeper subject, and nothing more impressive than what our life and society has in this one word. It holds four letters and encompasses its own mystique to which it is more like a phenomenon that everyone and no-one can explain. It is a word that has roots in Old English, Latin, Ancient Greek and Roman eras; as well as holds around 281 references in the Bible, if this Neanderthal could read the Koran, there is no doubt that it may be found there too. From the day we become a fertilized egg, this word is an embodiment of intrinsic meaning set as the strongest bond between a mother and her child; a feeling that embraces the very essence of the heart and soul. This one word that has been implemented and given so much power unto objects, people, and everyday life, portrays the best and worst emotions and feelings upon ourselves of which we have minimal to no control over. Yet there is no other word to take its place or use as an equal to leave such an impact upon the world. There are many differences in the way it is used. The word has been around for a very long time, maybe before Neanderthals; maybe as a grunt that transcended into what we know of it now. In fact, I believe that now in today's society the word has actually lost what it must have meant when it was first set and defined; but can this word really be defined to one way? I would say no; and we will explore this throughout.

The word we are embarking upon is not just a four letter word. It is embodied in the mind, spirit, feelings, emotion, bonds, ties and symbolically through our everyday lives. Whether good or bad, has held many symbols over the years and throughout the decades. Do yourself a favor as the reader -- if you know the word this Neanderthal is talking about, write down or draw two of your favorite symbols that represent this word in the margins. Why did you pick these symbols? Probably, between your life experiences and specific brain wiring, it is these types of symbols that have the most meaning to you in your life; for your version of what passion is. What is the correct symbol? The answer is whatever we allow the symbol to be; we chose items to represent what we believe to be the all empowering symbols of our embodiment of this word; no matter our religion or background, we all have that symbol that means so much to us. To some, the symbol chosen might be nothing more than a pile of sticks and mud. This pile may have been just the beginnings of a structure for a dwelling to keep the clan safe from harm; or a first feeling of embracing that instinct to protect the ones we care about. There are many symbols that we as a society use for this empowering word, but this Neanderthal is only going to touoh on a few of them.

The world has so many symbols for this word that a Modern Day Neanderthal has many to choose from. These symbols range from roses, knots, triangles, hearts, apples, four leaf clovers -- if you're Irish, arrows, the wings of a dove, cupids, hummingbirds and so many more. So what would a real Neanderthal of today think about all the different objects that represent this one impressive word that is only four letters? Would they be able to decipher the meaning of these specific symbols providing they already had some knowledge and understanding of the way each symbol is used? So how does one pick a symbol and know it is the right symbol for the correct meaning and situation? Would a Neanderthal be able to express the emotions depicted by way of an object, like we do for Hallmark holidays? Can the Neanderthal find someone that understands that same representation of the symbol chosen in the same way? Which one symbol do we find the best for our Modern Day Neanderthal?

For those of you homo-erectus who understand symbols, let's think about the fruit symbols, or at least the most commonly represented and known -- the apple. The apple was first talked about and has been described in the Bible, when Eve took it from the Forbidden Tree. Whether good or evil, it was a representation of the trust two people have in sharing and being as one as their journey began. As time, life and science move forward we learn from the myths and stories that our ancient ancestors left behind. From wall depictions to the interpreted language of time we have learned that many cultures sacrificed plentiful fruits such as grapes and apples to those Gods and Goddesses who were adorned to keep the piece or provide strength or belief among the people. The apple gets commonly used to describe or represent many sexual connotations as well as a brand that we know today. From the electronics to the clothing brand like Apple Bottom Jeans it is a statement and a symbol in our everyday society.

Mind Shaper: "I own a pair of those jeans!"

Neanderthal: "does it come with boots of the fur?"

Also, the apple is used to represent one person's endearment by stating that their partner is, "the apple of their eye." As an edible object, let's hope our Neanderthal is not hungry and misinterprets any butt or eyeball for an apple; because though eyeballs are full of nutrients for birds when we turn into carcasses, they are not quite the same as a Washington or Granny Smith. If the Neanderthal should choose to start biting said asses and eyeballs, we may have an epidemic of zombies running around. As another saying goes, an apple a day keeps the doctor away. So let's make sure to take care of ourselves first. Nurture yourself, respecting what's within before expressing emotions through symbols upon others. While our Modern Day Neanderthal tries to start hunting for his mate with fruit traps and not eating all the bait, there is only hope that he realizes that this is not the sole way to capture another's pulsing chest.

Mind Shaper: "What does that have to do with mere attraction towards others?"

Neanderthal: "Simple, it's just ONE of the many symbols. I mean, we can explore different symbols!"

Speaking of beating organs, the heart is the instrument of life much like the organ in a church on a Sunday sermon. The organ represents an endearing sound in churches and some baseball games, most of the time. Though the harp tends to be a much more romantically played instrument and could cause a mate to pay amorous attention to the Neanderthal, just like muses of the 1570s.[1] The harp is a symbol that has been considered an instrument to help with lyrics and poetics in the making of beautiful sounds that enchants the feelings of a wanted heart. In Norway, the harp has been considered a ladder to higher emotions of passion or a way to get to paradise. So a beautiful instrument for strumming could be used to tame the beast within, and would aid the Neanderthal in creating those sensual sounds of attracting a mate with more than snarls and grunts. But he needs to now learn how to play so it is not a sour note in creating such a passionate connection. The harp is sometimes also associated with Cupid (or the one who

---

[1]   (Venefica)

stabs us with that emotional feeling around that evil, Hallmark holiday, Valentine's Day), yet another confusing symbol for our Neanderthal. When he carries his arrows shooting those with the best intentions, it is in hopes of two people falling madly for each other. Or is this our own belief of Cupid trying to play practical jokes and actually causing us to fall, creating more emotional chaos?

Many humans, and in some instances, animals in the world, have used some natural earthly items that are considered to represent this word as a symbol in some form or another. Penguins show it by getting a pebble to their one life partner, yet we humans do the same with stones and a band around the one we believe is the truest.

Neanderthal: "Sometimes, the 'truest' can be found two or three times!"

Mind Shaper: "But sometimes you find THE one, and that's all you need!"

A couple of these other symbolic examples are the maple leaf or the beauty of the jasmine flower, if our Modern Day Neanderthal happened to have Hindu influences or ancestry among Asian, Chinese or European decent. The jasmine flower, a Hindu symbol that is represented throughout the Asian and Chinese cultures, holds a bit of modesty and certain attachment

11

feelings towards dear ones. This is much like when we use our olfactory senses and we know when we have arrived at grandma's house, or the smells of our favorite desserts. All of these experiences are representations of what this word means to us. While on the topic of nature, the maple leaf is another depiction in which we use as an object of adornment. The maple leaf was used by early American settlers and was carved into the foot of the bed to repent demons, encourage sexual pleasure and supposedly help with a peaceful night's sleep.[2] The leaf is also a symbol depicted in photos of storks carrying babies, maybe to ward off demons?

Neanderthal: "It makes you wonder about the Canadian flag -- could you replace the symbol with the word and have it mean the same?"

Mind Shaper: "Only a Neanderthal would try to change Canada's flag, the symbol of their country!"

Without picking nature or some random object, each person actually has a symbol and carries it with them at all times. In our modern everyday life we say "I heart you" with our hands in the shape of a heart out in front of us as if we took that shape right from our own chest. The shape of the human heart is more

---

[2]   (Venefica)

like the shape of our fist or even a weirdly shaped potato, but with the superior vena cava and aorta sticking out of it. The shape itself that we perceive and draw has stories and different meanings but has taken way as we know it over the years. The Silphium, an extinct plant, had seeds in the heart shape that we know and was the main ingredient in birth control of its time.[3] Historians believe this is one way that we have learned and adapted to the heart shape. As one of a few or many theories which try to explain the shape of the heart, the plant seems to be the most talked about, yet it cannot be proven that this is actually where the shape came from.

Another theory on where this symbolic shape came from is related to Aphrodite by way of the wings of a dove, well at least the back side of the dove. Good luck catching one to check the theory but holding one with wings together does make sense for the shape. Our Modern Day Neanderthal might be able to trap a dove and hand it to a perceivable mate. One more realistic theory is that the heart shape is modeled more closely to a cattle heart because it was more readily available to see than a human heart in past centuries. In medieval times, some artist depictions were botched or accidently misunderstood

---

[3]   (Cunningham)

when given a description of what a heart was to look like. So the cattle heart became a catalyst for representation. These are the offered theories for where the representation of the heart started. Others have even tried to pin the shape based on parts of the female body; of the breast, the buttocks and even the vulva; as the female pelvis also closely resembles a heart and it is where life is birthed and first perceived after conception. Many believe that this last theory of the womans body is the reason for the shape and that its meaning is one of adornment. If our Neanderthal now takes these different theories he will begin to understand how to use and treasure the symbols around. Whatever symbol he chooses to use will hopefully be used for an enduring courtship and not scare away any possibilities. This shape, the heart, has been perceived as the most acknowledged symbol over time; whether it be ancient, historical, modern or expressive the Modern Day Neanderthal now has this at his disposal.

Grrrrr nuuuuu hhhhhhhh booo mmmmm ssshhh aahh pth pth uuuuuug ckk ck ck. Or in other words, our Modern Day Neanderthal just threw his hands into the air and grunted. There are so many symbols, but the easiest thus far and most recognizable to our culture, is the hands shown into the shape of a heart; but it is good to know there are a lot of choices to decide from. That is just a scraping of the word through its symbols for you the Erectus, or Sapien, but remember these are minimal ideals with some facts about a word that comparatively still has so much more to offer. The Neanderthal of today would definitely be as confused, like so many of us humans, trying to learn how to show affection to any mate and figure out this most passionate of feelings; while learning which symbol is the best for us to use with this emotional embrace. Whether the Neanderthal is a Lufend or a Lufestre (that's male or female); they would have many choices as to which symbol would express their own feeling. Would they even understand the meaning of the word, or that the symbol they choose may be just be an irrational tie to their mate but has more meaning to themselves because of their proximity to each other; or would they just resort to their own natural primal instincts and not waste time on meaning, symbols, or words?

Can you see 14 symbols?

NeanderSong

This amazingly redundant word and its numerous symbols is just a sampling of many meanings for our Neanderthal but are the many variances thrown at us in everything we do within our very different facets of life. Bjjeerr gru mmmmb chunpa nawrrrr, or, "I am not sure which symbol;" groans our Modern Day Neanderthal as he sits and points to all that he sees as symbols for this word. It is hard, and almost crazy, to think of all the ways people interpret this one word or its meaning. The word is thrust into scripts, books, poems, song lyrics, websites and even our everyday language as a nonchalant way to describe something, or everything, we really, really like. Many homo erectus would be willing to possibly use a new word in everyday conversation; that is, if it had an equivalent. We hear the word so abundantly and don't even realize there are different meanings and levels of complication that comes along with it. In text or writing, for example, LOL could be a short funny hahaha or even a gut buster. It's hard to tell from the way it is written because text has no context, but that is how the word we use for romance is sometimes perceived. It is stated so many times, or brought to our attention so much, that it is as common as the words 'the', 'and', 'or' and 'it'; causing it to lose its context of believability and realism. When we hear it; the word has no deep meaning just subtle instances of life and reverberations. We know the many meanings from the literature and world around us whether songs, poems, books, movies or just someone saying it. This word for the longest time has taught us about its various forms with no real singular definition, without using the same word within its meaning. The word holds so much sway that sometimes it can just be a title of a song, or a sweet embrace; within the lyrics that we hear, but do not listen to. If we actually hear the lyrics that we are listening to, while playing our favorite songs, we can come to find the realizations of the good, bad, crazy, the romance, and even heartbroken endeavors that this one word can inhabit. The media of our time have propelled many Homo Erectus/ Sapiens to begin to understand the word and all of its glory, but in many thousands of different ways.

For the sake of the writings between these pages, some music has been played for this Neanderthal with a few chosen titles and some lyrics that might help describe this feeling in a song. It is believed to be stated that music can calm the savage beast, or if lucky enough, that beast may dance and howl with the sounds of a beating drum. "OOOCHA CHUCKA OOOCHA CHUCKA" as our Modern Day Neanderthal stomps about, and the rashness in his voice carries through the open air, he starts to learn about these songs. Now keep an open mind, and if you have some of these songs in your own playlist let them play gently in the background during this next section; and perhaps your inner Neanderthal or unsoothed beast will surface.

The songs in the next section have been randomly selected because they have the word in the title or chorus and encompass the range of feelings that this word can hold, sometimes all at once. Whether it is pain or cheer we know the songs and the meanings from being human, and to most of the population that's good enough. These are small samplings of regard for the word from this Neanderthal's life, trying to teach the next Neanderthal what this word is through all of its values. If we actually listen to and hear the songs, we can grow to learn these very meanings, and hope to use them in a different way in our lives. We yearn for the passionate relics of the past and seek the same emotions for whatever happens in the future. As well as our own selves, the Modern Day Neanderthal can learn the soul and heart of the lyrics in a song, and receive a glimmer of instance or chance to understanding another intrinsic meaning to this overly used word. Deep down, we catch ourselves singing some of the songs below as loudly as possible in our cars, showers or at a karaoke bar trying to express ourselves to a possible mate. These songs have had one word removed or changed, not to take away from the artist or their song, but to make the Neanderthal in all of us rethink this word in a new way; just to see how important the word is to our society. Below, is a poetic muse of lyrical contradictions using song titles to show how we are emotionally tied to the word.

> *The power of **Fervor**; but **Sympathy** don't cost a thing* so *What is **Amour**?*
> *I want to know what **Joy** is*....or even *Why do fools fall in **Regard**?*
> If ***Leubh** in any language* exist why is it a *Crazy little thing called **Ardor**?*
> In regards', *Whats **Fondness** got to do with it?* because if ***Eros** can build a bridge,* but you *Can't buy me **Passion*** then maybe I could purchase a ***Crush** potion #9.*

> Some say *All you need is **Compassion**,* but you have to *Give a little **Devotion*** to a *Dream **Paramour**,* or be lucky enough to have *Somebody to **Relish*** even if it is *Tainted **Lust**.* We choose to *Stop in the name of **Dislike*** because ***Fascination***

is a battlefield ;but in our minds **Affection** *will keep us together* if we just *Don't throw your* **Rapture** *away* like **Sex** *in an elevator.* Though fun *I* **Fancy** *rock and roll,* as a *Cradle of* **Ecstasy** especially since *I will do anything for* **Emotion.**

Is this **Weakness**? Because *Falling in* **Enjoyment** *with you* in a **Hump** *shack* has got me feeling like *I'll make* **Whoopee** *to you.* Do you *Feel like makin* **Hanky Panky** if I say *I can't stop* **Cherishing** *you. Can you feel the* **Heart** *tonight* if when we are together **Tenderness** *is what I got.*
I will always **Appreciate** *you;* especially *The way you* **Idolized** *me,* but *I think I* **Hate** *you.* **Enjoyment** *bites,* then *You've lost that* **Romantic** *feeling* and one says *Baby I need your* **Infatuation.**

I **Worship** *a rainy night,* but time surpasses and we start wondering *where did our* **Fling** *go? I just called to say I* **Like** *you;* when you **Adorn** *me tender, I can* **Agape** *you like that.* Then missing *How sweet it is to be* **Admired** *by you,* both could *Put a little* **Flame** *in your heart,* She may wonder if you *have* *you ever really **Desired** a woman.* He might know *She will be **Respected**. After the **Warmth** has gone,* we again search *All for **Devotion**;* in hopes of finding our one true **Soulmate**.

Neanderthal: "Hey Mind-shaper, could you imagine if this section was read by Christopher Walken?"

Mind Shaper: "Neanderthal, you have a lot of issues, but that was actually amusing can he use more cowbell!"

So if you read this poetic capture of items and realized that you know the title, the artist, or even the tune that could get stuck in your head, then your emotional ties to the word are still working and you are not dead. These words are all possibilities, but still can't represent the one word that is idolized. Let's say though, for our Neanderthal he/she still has no idea; better get him/her the best head phones and probably an iPhone with some of these items on shuffle, and see if that tames the beast within or makes them angry.

After doing an internet search for songs with the word in the title, and using nothing more than a thesaurus or dictionary, we can make our own titles of songs; but just as your eyes see them, your brain really wants you to say the word that belongs in that place. The word stems to have so many meanings and an understanding which we forget the L word is not just a simple word, and yet no other word makes any sense in the context or holds sentiment to one's heart. A few of these nonsense or brickabrack statements above could be combined to actually tell a story of a relationship or amorous courtship. While other written compilations, or combinations, could describe the good and bad and whatever of this word some seem there is none other than the Kings version of "*This Crazy Little Thing Called _ _ _ _.*"

So, per chance, here is one iota of an instance when five of the above mentioned songs are combined to describe this feeling, whatever it is. "I Want to Know What **Joy** is." "**Crush** Potion #9." "What's **Fondness** Got to do With it?" "Tainted **Lust**." and "**Fascination** is a Battlefield." Taking these five songs at random and debunking the word may just lend us to a bit more understanding of its powerful representation.

Foreigners' lines from "I want to know what **Joy** is" prior to the chorus are as follows:

> In my life there's been heartache and pain
>
> I don't know if I can face it again
>
> I can't stop now, I've traveled so far
>
> To change this lonely life [4]

---

[4]   (Foreigner, 1979)

23

Whoever decided upon these lyrics, states the problem of already being broken and the journey to get rid of the pain of this word; and its feelings that have caused one to be on a lonely path. When one is in a serious relationship and gets rejected, or is the rejecter, they more than likely suffer the heartache and pain that goes along with it. The way back to themselves, so they can move onto the next relationship, can be a lonely one if they don't seek help or talk it out with someone who cares. Many Homo Erectus/Sapiens though, when they hear that word, it means a quick fix to jump in the sack, say that silly little word, and make bad decisions; when in reality they haven't found what makes them feel that word for themselves instead of others.

Neanderthal: "Doesn't sex fix everything?"

Mind Shaper: "No you fool, it's just one act of abusing the word when you don't mean it!"

When, The Clovers or The Searchers are noticed on the local oldies radio station, a single song about a potion that would allow one to actually fall deeply for someone else does the trick just fine, because it seems to be a way that you can trick a person into more than just liking you. As intriguing as it is to this Neanderthal, we humans should wonder if The Clovers first researched and understood the chemicals in our brain that actually act as a potion sometimes. We still to this day do not know how to combine our own man-made chemicals that would fire in the same synopsis as the brains' natural chemicals to make us feel what this word is. Many state the word and feel it truly, but we have learned how to manipulate some of those feelings in our brain with extra Dopamine (the happy drug) or other medication because we are depressed. Anyways, the Clovers lyrics are:

> It smelled like turpentine, it looked like Indian ink
> I held my nose, I closed my eyes, I took a drink
> I didn't know if it was day or night
> I started kissin' everything in sight
> But when I kissed a cop down on Thirty-Fourth and Vine
> He broke my little bottle of L--- Potion Number Nine[5]

It is very interesting that over decades of years, voodoo doctors, shaman, and various cultures believe that certain ritual dances, or ceremonial gifts, could help with the cause of connecting two beings as one. The idea of an actual potion

---

[5] (Clovers, 1959)

made from simple spices causing an arousal in one mate, or a sense of lust in others, is interesting, especially since it might not be chocolate, strawberry or any other normal aphrodisiac we could think of. In due facts, the feeling and emotion could take time; but also passes because of chemicals in our brain that do not allow us to be in a state of euphoric emotion forever, because we would build immunities to them and lose that feeling. Once the brain is involved, the rest of the body also tends to be stimulated or produces perspiration, things that may or may not show to those we seek as a suitor. The pupils dilate, the heart races, and sometimes the words we speak make no cohesiveness at all because of the L word and the confusion it brings. Many singers and songwriters describe the heart in their version of passion or amorous feelings toward another. Tina Turner has such a voice to exploit this element of the body when she sings in *"What's **Fondness** Got To Do With It."* She sings as if she would have had more control in her own heart if she had kept her fondness for herself and not given it away, letting this silly word go when dealing with her personal dramas. The problem is that no one can control what our heart wants when we want it or need it; that feeling just happens, so below are her tears in writing:

Who needs a heart when a heart can be broken?

Then she goes on a state about the confusion and for whatever reason she cannot figure it out.

You do it for me oh oh oh

What's Fondness Got To Do with It[6]

Without knowing, and like so many people throughout the world, we have grand ideas of what the reasons are that one gets extremely attracted to another; whether it is looks, money, personality, brains, attitude and/or a handful of other items that attribute to mating while learning to be with someone. What we do not know is how such a strong bond connects through our hearts. This bond is driven by our brain and gets mixed in with the heart and hurts deep inside when we get "broken." The words Tina speaks in this song resonate and hints to everyone listening that it is normal to be confused when someone is enamored by another, and that you must be ready to feel pain. The brain and body tend to work and fight against each other in a win-win, lose-lose type of deal when we choose to get lost in the emotions this word creates when trying to find decent suitors.

The group *Soft Cell* mentions a bit of the craziness that comes with the lust and romance within the heart, in any

---

[6]   (Turner, 1984)

given moment. Most recently, some other intriguing people of society have covered this catchy tune. You may have heard the original, but may also only know the version done by *Marilyn Manson*. Most singles, though practicing coitus, tend to forget connecting with mind, body, and soul as they try to become romantically involved, making it nothing more than "**Tainted Lust**". Sometimes, it is okay to run from, be scared of, and even enjoy what may be right or wrong at that moment in time; it is tainted, not quite right, and there is no answer as to why.

Once I ran to you (I ran)
Now I'll run from you
This tainted **Lust** you've given
I give you all a boy could give you
Take my tears and that's not nearly all
Oh...tainted **Lust**

Then a bunch of more lines before mentioning it again something like this.

And you think _____ is to pray
But I'm sorry I don't pray that way[7]

---

[7]   (Cobb, 1981)

Let it be man to man, woman to woman, man to woman, or any other different combination of one's choosing, this song says that lust is tainted. First, yearning for the other so they run to each other, but the pain of the infatuation causes them to hurt each other and the only thing to do is run away; almost out of sight out of mind. The craziness of no sleep at night because of that very obsessive trait we show when we really are enamored with someone, or crazy in lust, is enough to drive us to insanity. Then later in the song, the rejecter doesn't want to make it right or remain friends (they need their space); but the rejecter has already moved on to new pursuits to hold others tight, making the rejected feel sorry and disappointed, but not to be preyed upon; like the heart which is now broken by the rejecter.

This is as true as heartbreak can get in some people; they vie for the compassion of another, but sometimes are not ready to show the same compassion because it's bad timing and just not meant to be, yet The realization is that they might not have taken that chance at the right moment, then life happens and they realize they waited too long. The courtship of the two in the song, probably during the romantic phase, was more a necessity for the two because of their primal instincts that take over and that the relationship felt comfortable and familiar. The running from the other, or the pain within, becomes the last resort; but the easiest to accomplish because if they could just run away from each other, they might just become friends again and get rid of those feelings of amore. The friendship they once had will never be as strong as the bond when they fell in smitten with each other, but the feelings of the heart and brain are always different with every person and show very similar characteristics throughout the years.

The feelings and actions caused by this word are so confusing, that even the Modern Day Neanderthal will have to suffer like everyone else; and just figure out this monstrous addicting drug and it's crazy feeling in the battlefield of life. Oh, by the way, Pat Benatar, in 1983, released this single that hit the top of the charts; and even though the words might have been written by others, she made it have a feeling and understanding of the despair and joy that this word can bring. The back and forth between two sweethearts can really feel like one is at war, either with themselves or with the other. The emotional roller coaster of raised happiness and saddened situations is the battlefield in which we all suffer through; getting to the state of being attached, or just not attracted to. The battlefield below helps a little with that back and forth:

You're begging me to go

Then making me stay

Why do you hurt me so bad

It would help me to know

Do I stand in your way

Or am I the best thing you've had

This is a typical kind of relationship when it seems so back and forth with young hearts.

Fascination is a battlefield

In all relationships -- young, experienced, broken or not, it becomes a battlefield to decide if being together or being apart is best for them; but it hurts them to be apart and being together is much like being on a high that will crash if they are not together. "IT," not the movie, but as an emotional state and concentrated being, within the realm that is felt, can feel like you are trapped or chained to another without your own individual personality. Due to the fear there will be no one else or that the situation is possibly sour; this causes people to question themselves as well as what will happen if the other one goes away? It is the chance every relationship starts out with, even though on the outside everything seems normal. It is the battlefield within ourselves to figure out which grass is greener, or feelings are the deepest; what this emotion is, or how we truly feel about someone. Though in the end we are strong beings searching for the right fit (even if its young puppy-like lust); no one will be able to stop it or even say one should or should not take the chance to let ones' self feel the heartache that comes with such an emotion.

These songs, along with so many others, have a great Erato, or muse, telling a worthwhile story and it is the expression of feelings we take from them to understand this insane word. The emotions that come with this powerful word extend through writings even before Shakespeare, Darwin, Plato and the mythology of the many countries of the world. As we listen to songs and hear the meanings they have, we get a sense of emotion towards those we really care about. Break-up songs are the worst; they are what seems to be the songs on the radio or your everyday world that happen per chance of a loss or gain of extreme feelings towards another. We miss them, we want them, and we want them to hold us like the words in the songs (even if it brings heartache); because it is that strong of an emotion and without that crazy feeling we tend to feel empty or lost.

No matter how the word, emotion or feeling seems to be portrayed in songs, the media or in our daily lives; the truth is that when we don't need it, we want it; but if we want it, we become needy for it and the lust, infatuation and desire take over. When we really hear these words and listen to them with more than our ears, we understand the adoration and emotional roller coaster that these very pulses thrive for another being. The chances we take to find that special someone include unknowingly that heartache, pain, deflated emotions and loss of heart could happen, but we do not live for the bad things that could happen; we choose to find a compliment or a challenge in which we think will make us a better person. Though our poor Neanderthal may not yet know what it is like to be broken from within, he will learn through nature itself because it is a crazy song and dance that cannot be stopped or forced, just happens when it happens, sometimes out of nowhere.

Neanderthal: "Oh, that's so deep! I never knew a song could have so many feelings!"

Mind Shaper: "I told you, there are numerous explanations within how you say that word."

Neanderthal: "I am starting to see that now, but I'm still extremely confused."

Mind Shaper: "That's okay. All of our real-life experiences lead into other stories about what this word is."

Neanderloss

......a short story

The Neanderthal in this story was a modern day alpha male to those who knew him; he was kind, caring, hard-working, and well... a player to some in the game of finding a true mate. The Neanderthal himself chose to never really let anyone get closer to him, more than just a friend or work acquaintance. Though the Neanderthal had a close group of friends whom he could confide in and always count on, they still only knew him as the funny, crazy, can't back down from a challenge and do anything he wants kind of guy. Many thought of him as the goofball, an over achiever or even the guy that some girls would be jealous of not having in their lives because he stood up for them and liked being a protector. But he perfected the ability to not let anyone in, or get too close, until one summer when the Neanderthal met a beautiful being, called the Artist.

The Artist, a beautiful, wild, spitfire of whom those who knew her would say she accepted challenges, had such a passion for her job and growing skills and really enjoyed just living life to the fullest. The Artist had a sweet disposition and a great spirit for laughter in a crowd; she too was considered to have dominance amongst other females, making them jealous of her and her accomplishments. She chose to push others away because she wanted to strive to achieve her own goals, but she did not close herself off to the chance at something more. In fact, during the first meeting between her and the Neanderthal, many would have thought they had known each other for a very long time.

The two had been hired for a summer near the east coast, but had never met in person until work started. The working environment was much like camp mixed with some crazy chaos and long hours. The Neanderthal had introduced himself first through emails as the Artist's direct boss; while getting responses from everyone, hers stuck out to him from the beginning, as excitement in her language and the chance at a new job and possibility. The first day of work was a day of introductions and learning what skills people had, almost like the first day of school. After a couple days the Neanderthal and the Artist crossed paths in the mess hall along with a few others but this was the first real interaction the two had not directly related to work.

Over a short amount of time both had become smitten by each other's presence. The first couple weeks the Neanderthal and the Artist found themselves hanging out more and talking about anything and everything about the world, including their work. Both were quick to realize that each of their previous relationships were over and done and they had decided to take a chance with each other, even though neither thought that it would be anything more than a great summer with a really cool person. The summer offered them a chance to work together and blossom into a romance that everyone seemed to think skipped all the way to being part of attachment amour, and not just puppy passion.

One thing that helped these two birds become one was their close proximity (which is one proven way that people become close), sharing things, life and experiences (which is generally why people fall for each other), and the little nuances in life. Over the whole summer they learned how to separate work and play and only squabbled about silly small things. The two had encountered one altercation; which started over a party and bad decisions due to being young and dumb. It is part of life and growing, learning each other and realizing what it takes to be in a relationship.

The Neanderthal, not thinking during this party where everyone was drinking and having a good time, decided to kiss the birthday girl's head and hold her tight in an embrace for her celebration and nothing more. The birthday girl was sad that her sudo-boyfriend at the time was hanging out with the Artist instead of her; and the Neanderthal figured comforting her was the best thing to do at the time considering he was not worried about the Artist hanging out with someone else. The next day, the green eyed jealousy monster and incorrect rumors got attached to the Artist who became furious at the Neanderthal for his actions, questioning the rumors that he did more than what actually happened. The Neanderthal, like a typical man, almost destroyed anything he had with the Artist and did not even realize it. The Artist was not about to be treated like that, and was not going to put up with anyone acting the way the Neanderthal did. In her angered retaliation, the Artist put her tennis shoes on, in the afternoon, shortly after work, and just ran as far away as possible because of some misinterpreted grapevine information. The Neanderthal, just minutes after finding out she ran, dropped what work related projects he was doing and decided that she meant more to him than anything else, and ran after her. Angry at himself for not being able to tell the Artist what happened, he dashed past others asking which way she went, and they all pointed towards the direction where there was a fork in the road nearly blocks away. He dug deep, and at full sprint, ran towards the fork in the road in hopes of chasing and catching up to this one being that his heart was beating and yearning for.

The universe must have been rooting for a challenge for these two because as the Neanderthal ran up to the fork in the road, there was no Artist in sight. With nothing more than a choice of left, right or just give up the chase, that day the Neanderthal didn't hesitate his decision to run as hard as he could to one side of the fork, in hopes of not going down the wrong side. Luckily, about three quarters of a mile down the winding road was both the best and worst the Neanderthal hoped to find, a woman of radiance and beauty pissed off and angrily sweating out tears ready to tear off his head. It may have been fate, strong electrical energy, or just the universe letting things happen; then again maybe it was a beautiful accident.

The Neanderthal caught up to the Artist in hopes of a conversation and a second chance to say he was sorry and explain himself. Once the run ceased they started walking and discussed the situation; both pleading their case. That night, when spending time apart, the universal wavelengths cohesively enhanced their relationship to an even stronger bond than just friends or summer mates; they started falling for each other. The Neanderthal, until this summer, had never met anyone that held such a spark or the right symmetry of the face as the Artist to his endangered heart. The Artist had not yet met a Neanderthal that had so much positive energy and such a sense of danger and protection at the same time; so for these two beings it was just right for them to meet.

A few weeks later, during a very busy time, the two shared some laughs and a bit of anger over a silly bowl of chili, which he would not eat because he was being stubborn and only focusing on work. The Artist got it for him just trying to make sure he ate and take care of him considering he would not do it himself. The Neanderthal was not used to someone caring so much as to bring him a bowl of chili, he was used to being the lone wolf; still he ate it and eventually pleaded forgiveness. The two, after reconciling, realized the situation was funny, at most, and not worth a real argumental blow up, but it did take awhile for them to understand that.

Mind Shaper: "Stupid boys! Sometimes women just want to take care of their men!"

Neanderthal: "That's silly, but it sounded like he was busy. I guess he should have just said thank you!"

Mind Shaper: "Probably."

The summer for these two was long due to the work load but extremely short due to the schedule and the Neanderthal's commitments to get back to school to finish his education.

Enamored with thoughts that neither had a definite idea of what was to come, the moment of excitement seemed right for the Neanderthal to ask the Artist to take a chance at the end of the summer to get in her vehicle and follow him to his residence, which was many states away from everything she knew, including family and friends. The Neanderthal did not mean to just take her away from everything, but wanted to start the next steps in the crazy obstacles of starting a new life; and at that very moment he didn't want to live a day without her. The two stayed in touch until the ending of the summer job as they were states apart, but as she packed her car at the end of that summer she decided to take the a scary chance and possibly the most wild journey, ever.

Five states later, and one new time zone, the Artist ended up accepting the challenge to take the chance of adventure with the Neanderthal. On a brisk fall morning, the Neanderthal woke to a phone call from the Artist, in tears, saying, "Good Morning. I am lost and not sure where I am".

The long drive had caused a small bit of misdirection, but the Artist was ecstatic to hear the Neanderthal's voice as he helped her get to a road amongst cornfields, nearly 30 miles away from his house. Knowing the distance she had traveled, the Neanderthal jumped upon his feet, got into his vehicle, and with no mind of the speed hurried out to meet her. She had driven through the night and the Neanderthal excitedly drove more distance in a few minutes than what seemed possible. But the two of them managed to drive up on each other with dust flying up as the Neanderthal and Artist slammed on their breaks into a gravel drive on the side of the road. Both emerged from their respective vehicles and held each other in the strongest embrace possible, as if they hadn't seen each other in years, even though it had only been a few weeks. Their eyes met, hearts were pounding and the kiss shared was filled with so much passion. Both hearts as one, and both enamored with being the puzzle piece that completed the other's missing parts in their own lives.

Over a few months, the Artist and Neanderthal spent all of their spare time together when he wasn't at school. She found in herself that she needed her own outlet, which in turn became an adventure for tho two of them. She was able to find another location to practice her craft; it just happened to be about 8 hrs away in yet another place which neither had been to. She accepted the gig and realized that the Neanderthal was going to be able to get a winter internship at the very place where she was going to practice her craft. They again got to spend work time and home life together. After the internship the Neanderthal returned to school while the Artist kept at her job, which caused a struggle due to irreconcilable differences and safety concerns with her direct boss. When trouble started for the Artist, the Neanderthal stated, "Come home if it's that bad there." In the matter of a few conversations the Artist and Neanderthal came together again as home became the arms of each other for safety and strength.

The two had come to some weird realization that doing things together, whether work or just going for walks became their mode in trusting and understanding each other. They had become one as by choice but both still had themselves as well but many saw these two as inseparable. By the end of the Neanderthal's school year the two had managed to find a new place that they both could practice their craft together for another summer before the artist got motivated to get more educated. These two seemed to work well together and not take work drama home most of the time; but the new place would challenge them almost as much as the trials and craziness to get there. They had hundreds of miles to get to the new destination and within an hour into the journey they both found themselves on the side of the road dealing with one of life's real problems- a flat tire because of a giant piece of lumber that literally attacked the vehicles, causing the Artist to run over it and flatten her driver's side wheel. It took some time but with the help of a stranger they were able to switch to the donut and keep on traveling to their new destination. They drove through many states; had a few small stops along the way and a couple of crazy weather storms, but managed to get to their new summer mountain location to start work.

It was another summer that had them each in charge of each other at different times of the day, yet at the end of the day they would try to hang out and enjoy each other. When you work that closely to each other there is bound to be some tension and stress build up. Over the time they had spent together, they had learned to appreciate each other's company in the close proximity of work, and union compatibility when outside of work. One evening, after stressful hours of work, a stake was driven slightly between the two. With a close friend of the Neanderthal's showing up to hang out, a bon fire with camaraderie and banter pursued. Due to a snide comment to the Artist from the Neanderthal's friend, she became enraged because the Neanderthal did not stick up for her. The Neanderthal and the Artist disagreed about that evening for a long time. Was the Neanderthal in the wrong? Probably, since his manners were thrown out the window for not sticking up for his Artist and being a dumb guy by not saying anything to his friend. She felt uncomfortable and mentioned it to the Neanderthal, but instead he told his friend that what he did was rude and then shrugged it off as nothing more than a thought. The Artist didn't see it that way, and with all the rest of the stress that was around at the time, it became the biggest obstacle that they needed to work through thus far in their relationship.

Mind Shaper: "Again, I will say, stupid boy for ignoring her feelings!"

Neanderthal: "Maybe it's her fault for not directly communicating her anger."

Mind Shaper: "Maybe it's his for not actually standing up for his girl!"

Neanderthal: "We boys can't read minds!"

Mind Shaper: "Why not you should be able to?"

The summer went on with a lot of hard work and the idea that, at the end of summer the two would again drive together back towards one of the oldest cities on the east coast so the Artist could have a chance to accomplish and further her education. For the first, time the chance of adventure coincided within the Artist letting the Neanderthal follow her as she took the wheel at the helm. It was a chance that both could follow goals; but would allow the Artist to follow her dreams a bit more, unlike before when she left everything else behind to join up with the Neanderthal for his dreams.

The two soul mates had built a very strong bond over work and free time so the new challenge back on the other side of the country was expected to be an interesting one. Once the two arrived, school started up quickly for the Artist while the Neanderthal searched for work. The time these two spent together started dwindling due to the business of each day, stress took over and work was hard to get in the good ole boy network. The Neanderthal and the Artist were slipping away from each other. Both tried to be there for the other, but they had lost themselves making each other more irritated and confused about the world. The Neanderthal and the Artist stopped doing things together like they had for their whole relationship; yet they still had this extremely intense bond that they kept coming back to. These two had never felt or gone through a super rough patch in the whole time they had been together. They always seemed to bounce back to each other, but with all the stress of school and lack of work, it made it difficult until that weird Hallmark holiday when the Neanderthal tried to show his romantic side.

Instead of wasting money for that Hallmark holiday, the Neanderthal decided to create something from the heart.

He wrote a letter out of candy hearts that was a romantic gesture which almost asked the Artist to be with him as his life partner; but the actual words were not uttered, just represented. This made the Artist almost glow and it enhanced the feeling between the two, but that was short lived and might have caused a distraction which the Artist wasn't ready for because of her overworked school load. As school was coming to an end for the year, the two had started to slip away from each other because the Neanderthal had gotten a job in yet another location, and the Artist wanted to go back home because she was homesick. This was the time where their proximity was challenged, and they took on even more stress trying to juggle a long-distance relationship. Finding the balance between work and his relationship with the Artist, became the Neanderthal's obsession; but unfortunately work still remained his mistress, no matter what. Neither said goodbye because that is forever, but they started wandering from each other as life took over.

That's where proximity is important for these two, much like many relationships. The two had spent so much time together that time apart is what drove these beings from the feelings they had for each other from the beginning. Emotionally, these two grew apart because the Artist started falling for a fantasy of some other homo sapian; hoping that the grass would be greener on the other side because she was working so close with him, and not the Neanderthal. The Neanderthal made the decision to only put work first; and didn't appreciate the time the Artist tried to put in when they first parted, so inevitably she would fall for the one closest to her. When they first parted ways, the Neanderthal chose to create a romantic game, which in turn would have led the Artist to either saying yes or no fourteen months from the day the Neanderthal chose work over her. Little did he know, the Artist was not about playing more games, and this only caused more tension between the two.

In the middle of that summer, the Neanderthal and the Artist had decided that their time together had finally come to an end, by way of a couple phone calls, a few emails, and even one last visit. Their paths were no longer coinciding and they felt it best to remain friends, but nothing more because they actually had grown away from the deepest compassion that they once had for each other. The game had ended and new challenges faced the two of them just not together.

Nonetheless, the Neanderthal was still in high hopes that he would be able to win back his Artist if he never gave up. Over time, the Neanderthal moved on but never forgot about the Artist and the great time and adventures the two had. He kept her in his mind, heart and even his pocket for awhile even when others were around maybe in hopes of someday being reunited. The Artist did the opposite and stored all the memories in a box; put it away in a closet to hopefully forget any of the bad that may have been between the two "birds" since they truly were enamored one time with each other. Both felt empty whenever something reminded them of the good times, but understood that those good memories were everlasting and could never change at the moment that they had happened. When the two first grew apart they may have both suffered from what some studies consider frustration attraction due to the fact that they might still have had feelings of that four letter word for the other; but both also felt that bit of rejection because neither was right or wrong, just different and not together anymore. They parted, but it took a while and both decided to just be admirable to each other as they grew and started following whatever dreams they happened to chase for themselves.

For years afterward, the Neanderthal tried and tried to regain what he had lost with his Artist with a lot of different people and ideals but struggled finding what he deemed to be truest or someone whom was his soul mate, but he struggled alone. The Artist went her own way and found many of her own struggles mostly trying to find herself. She had gone from someone to something in hopes of also finding that right puzzle piece. The Artist and The Neanderthal, both runners of sorts, ran from their own feelings into the arms of others or to work to make it so that each other became out of sight out of mind to the other. The two beings try to chat from time to time and pick up with their friendship and conversations right where they left off before their worlds turned upside down, just only with more hesitation in their voices and a mere calmness about life.

The two may never have the chance to be together again; but what they had cannot really be explained, nor can anything harm the friendship they first created before the Neanderthal and the Artist first said that silly four letter word to each other. They meant it when they said it and it was a beautiful connection, but things change. What a mysterious piece of magic these two shared, as if they believed they were true soul mates; yet life put obstacles in their way so they would have trouble being together. Proximity became their main means of true compassion for each other over their years together, along with many other items just like so many relationships. Over time, separation and different journeys they grew apart; but the initial friendship and companionship these two shared was through mind, body, heart and soul. It was a magical (almost sickening, how cute it was) amore that could be unstoppable when the two were together. Many relationships go through many stages from the excitement, to struggle, to happiness and even frustration; sometimes a lot more but each connection is something that will either grow through everything or grow apart. The Artist and the Neanderthal experienced the beauty and the sadness this word can have even with such a small timeline.

Neanderthal: "So you can actually enjoy someone even after you've grown apart? That's weird!"

Mind Shaper: "One's endearment for their first can last a lifetime, but it's the experiences you take out of it that make you stronger and teach you about this word!"

Neanderthal: "Will it ever go away?"

Mind Shaper: "No, it changes, grows, and challenges you! In fact, men and women change every day, as does that emotion."

Neanderthal: "Then show me the way, oh Mind Shaper!"

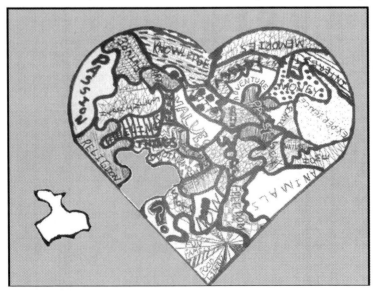

Brainderthal?

Or is it really Neanderheart?

Mind Shaper: "Fine, I will Neanderthal!"

Let me start this chapter with a little bit of a disclaimer, this chapter is sternly written with the female perspective in mind. This writing is from personal experiences as a semi Neanderthal's wife, and hopes to impart some understanding or wisdom. However, that does not mean that current Neanderthals are above this chapter. In fact, it is essential that you experience the mysteries of the female mind that may intrigue and be unveiled here. Ok, maybe that was a bit overly dramatic for what this is... let's try again. Guys, this chapter is a different perspective for you because it is important for you know what your girl might have going on in her brain and possibly what we expect from you. Better? Also, don't get all putted up about gonder roles here, in this section there is a more traditional stance on the experience of emotions towards another. That does not mean that I'm anti-feminism, because trust me I am not; however, a Neanderthal by definition fits the "traditional" masculine male role which we are pertaining to within our writing.

Neanderthal: "Wait, I'm supposed to pay attention to this?"

Mind Shaper: "Yes, you are the Neanderthal, pay attention!"

So...How do you know your man is a Neanderthal?

Not every man out there qualifies as a Neanderthal. In fact, I would say in a mild opinion that as a society we have started moving away from this type of male role, and towards a more progressive male image. A more Ken doll meets societal lumberjack, but without the skills that men once possessed which seemed to make them manly and protective. That is not saying that society is not trying to make the new lumbersexuals or hipsters into Neanderthals, but they also do not quite qualify to be that of a Modern Day Neanderthal. This is evident in the media, because we are seeing less of the John Wayne, Charles Bronson, Sylvester Stallone type of characters in movies and less Tim Allen, Bob Villa, types on television. We are experiencing more sensitive or "softer" characters, or thuggish embellishments instead of manly men. That's not saying that men can't be sensitive or that there is anything wrong with this type of man. A lot of the time they can seem like a bunch of egotistical asses or like they have lost their own instinct which makes them savage and protective, which women do sometimes find attractive. From thug-like appearances to effeminate men it seems as if they make a decent living but have none of those manly qualities about them like being able to change a tire, hunt or fish. The modern progressive male gives the image of a sensitive, nurturing man; but our boys are growing up soft. As culture has shifted away from the image of what was the "traditional man," or Neanderthal man, we see men now changing more with culture and what society wants instead of treading their own path. This makes finding a Modern Day Neanderthal man even harder to find as it is becoming more socially acceptable to be less "manly."

In the Neanderthal's Brain

The typical Neanderthal is a unique and rare breed because he fits into a traditional role in a variety of ways. He shows his caring through his action by protecting and providing for his companions. The part of the brain that corresponds to protection, tho dorsal premammillary nucleus, is larger in the male brain than the female, and this portion of the brain is wired to detect challenges by other males and environmental dangers.[8] Though, with females, response to dangerous situations happens through (more often than not) hormonal

---

[8]   (Brizendine, 2010)

imbalances and usually are expressed when she becomes enraged because something bad has happened to the ones they care about; most likely their young. This "Momma Bear Syndrome." as I like to think about it, is the protection of one's cubs. Much like the typical male with his clan or family, the female is with her cubs; without the extra hormones, just instincts.

The amygdala, which is responsible for responding to threats, fear and danger, is also relatively larger in a man's brain[9] than a woman's. Not saying men have bigger brains, they just don't use them the same way women do and vice versa. The amygdala, also is the part of the brain which controls sexual arousal and sends messages throughout the body. However, this emotional word which we use to get the feelings associated with it activates or initiates areas of the brain with a high concentration of receptors for Dopamine and Norepinephrine which are associated with euphoria, craving, and addiction.[10] With these chemicals, the brain experiences lust and infatuation differently. Erotic photos stimulate lust and activate the hypothalamus, which controls hunger and thirst; and for your brain, lust tends to be a short-term sensation and

---

[9]   (Brizendine, 2010)

[10]   (Cohen, 2007)

the stronger emotions they can be considered an addiction. As yuck and stereotypical as it sounds, you are his addiction on the deepest animal level. You, the female of the male's choosing, are his territory and he is biologically inclined to protect you and what kin you may have. This doesn't mean that he should be like a barking Chihuahua at its kibble bowl; he just wants you to be safe and well cared for!

This is different from our female brains because the part of the brain that controls emotional empathy, the mirror neuron system, is larger in the female brain. This is why girls are typically more in tune with the emotions and non-verbal cues of others. Interestingly enough, in men's brains, emotional reactions initially can be much stronger than a female's. For example, when a man experiences emotional pain his face can change to hide true emotion. In about 2.5 seconds his face changes without him even registering the change. Poker anyone? The female's body language, along with facial reactions, are seen more easily; but are also hidden because their brain allows the ease of differences, where men are wired to hide anything because it does not make them seem manly enough; though both sexes do have the ability to express many emotions just by way of their body language.

Body language makes those moments of "I'm fine!" a relationship nightmare for the Neanderthal! You know exactly what I mean ladies, when you say you're furious but you respond with an angry "I'M FINE!" I know that in my mind all I can think is, "Can't he tell I'm furious? I sound so angry, my arms are crossed, my hip is shifted! What is wrong with him? Doesn't he care?" repeat for the next 20 minutes until finally bursting into tears. In his mind it's something like, "Hmm, she says she's fine, okay then," until 20 minutes later when the female bursts into tears and he's ambushed by an angry, hurt and sobbing woman! The even crazier part of this happens inside the female brain. As we become more and more upset, the rational part of our mind is screaming that we are being irrational and crazy; but can't seem to pull ourselves back from the edge. It's a bizarre experience that takes years to control if we learn how to.

Neanderthal: "So you're saying women are crazier?"

Mind Shaper: "Yes, you just need to deal with it!"

Neanderthal: "It's no wonder we'll never figure you women out!"

Mind Shaper: "It's science. It's her brain waves. They're different."

What you really need to understand during your meltdown, is that it is not his fault if he does not comprehend you, or your emotional state. Men by nature, think about what someone else may do in a situation; whereas females typically think about how others would feel. This doing attitude is what causes him to want to fix things for you. The fancy technical name for this is action-empathy.[11] The exchange below is a classic instance of feeling vs. doing.

> **Her**: Oh, my gosh! I had the worst possible thing happen to me today! I forgot my bag this morning and the papers I needed for my presentation were in there! It was so embarrassing, I looked like an idiot!
>
> **Him**: Well, you could have just ran back home for them?
>
> **Her**: Seriously? I would have been so late, that would have been worse!! I had to reschedule the whole thing for tomorrow!!
>
> **Him**: Well, why don't you put your bag in the car now so you don't forget it tomorrow?

---

[11]   (Levant, 1992)

Her: NO! *screaming* Are you even listening to me?! I was so embarrassed and now you are making me sound stupid! You are treating me like a child! I am not stupid! You think you are smarter than me, don't you!!!

Him: *Dumbfounded* What just happened?

Poor guy, he was trying in his way to help out by suggesting some things that might have solved her problem. She feels like he's not even listening to how embarrassed and upset she was. Men want to fix your problems because they don't want you to be hurt or upset. It's part of his primal desire to protect you![12] Now, the easiest way to keep situations like this from escalating, are to preface the conversation by explaining to your Neanderthal that you just need to vent and that you just want him to listen to you. Men, that means it's time to just sit on your hands, listen, and offer responses like, "wow, that sucks!" Commiserate her but don't be condescending. Ladies, if you do this before you are about to blow up, you can count on having a pretty good set of ears for yourself!

Next, like most males, animals included, he is a very visual, visceral creature and the brain works as a compartmentalized

---

[12]   (Gregor, 1987)

memory bank pulling from all experiences. This part of my section to you, the reader, is going to really irk some of your ladies; I'm sorry but it is scientifically proven, stick with me here! When a man sees a woman their brain is subconsciously looking for a fertile mate. In fact, men in amore actually show more activity in the parts of the brain that process visual stimuli.[13] Whether it is the symmetry of the face or the pear shaped body that visually appeals to a man, subconsciously he is looking to find the best of what he sees as a possible mate. The creature world is very apt to this, as well as many species, and they use songs, dances or even showings of strength to find the correct mate. In fact, the females of the world do it too, much like the creature world only with make-up, dressing the right or wrong way, and inviting friends along on outings to see if the male is the right fit.

Anthropologically, fertility in a woman equals bigger breasts and wide hips; is it any wonder that most men are visually attracted to women's curves? It's not that he is actively pursuing a new mate (and men don't even try that as an excuse!) Ok fine, I get it men are seeking something that is perfect in their eyes, but so are women. I enjoy how Brizendine describes it;

---

[13]   (Cohen, 2007)

she says that, "men look at attractive women the way we look at pretty butterflies. They catch the male brain's attention for a second, but then they flit out of his mind."[14] So ladies, this means that your Neanderthal is going to look at women the way we look at art. It's not that he's trying to make you feel jealous or inadequate. In my opinion this is a CALM conversation you should have with your Neanderthal. If it bothers you, you should speak up CALMLY and explain to him why, and what your concerns are. However, I hate to burst your bubble, but I highly doubt it is something you will be able to change. In my own relationship I accept that there are other women in the world that my husband finds attractive, and in all honesty there are other men in the world that I think are also attractive, (hello Chris Pratt, I'm talking about you sir)... However, I have no concern that he will pursue them, because by nature the true Neanderthal is loyal to his own clan. Along with a Neanderthal being loyal, the other thing you need to understand, ladies, is that when your Neanderthal is truly attracted to you, he looks at you with greater attraction than any other female, even Jennifer Lawrence.

---

[14]   (Brizendine, 2010)

How He Shows Affection

Along with this, typically a man shows his affection with actions, not with words. We women show our men we are enthralled by them in those mushy ways, and we think our guys should do the exact same thing; but remember your man's brain does not work like yours! As women, we judge our men based on how we think they should show their affection towards us. Watch any romance movie and you'll see the female perspective of romance in some big grand way. Let your Neanderthal show you in his way; even if that means a kiss on the forehead, him holding your hand while walking in public, or some other gesture comfortable to him, and enjoy it. When men are ready, they will express more openly how they actually feel about you; but it may take time to understand what you want, need, and desire.

Neanderthal: "Why can't you girls just tell us what you want?"

Mind Shaper: "We try to tell you what we want, but then you men think we are trying to change you."

Neanderthal: "But you tend to change us."

Mind Shaper: "We hope for the good and not the bad. It's not that we want to try and change you, but we want to feel what they do in the movies."

Neanderthal: "The movies are not as real as what we are; we all just show it in a different way!"

My own example of this is something that bothered me for quite a while; and in true womanly fashion I was annoyed about it for weeks before I bit the bullet and just asked. Every night before my significant other and I go to sleep, most of the time before I hang up the phone, and at other random times I tell my Neanderthal that I adore him, by using the word we are not using in this book. The only time I consistently get a response is before we go to sleep, and that's when I get a "me too," usually in a grunt. When I asked him about it his response was simple, he knows that I admire all of him and I know he the same. It's a given, period, end of conversation, moving on with life.

It's a statistical fact that both men and women use the word, but men have generally been known to say it first as a subconscious way of stating that the female is his.

Though the male will also be skeptical to say it more readily than the female because, in retrospect, he is afraid of losing what masculinity he feels he has left, after being vulnerable enough to use this word first. He is wired to be more of a quiet non-verbal, maybe even non-physical type... (Yes this is just as confusing as we females whenever we have an argument). One of the first things he is going to do when he wants to be in a relationship with you, is let the other people in his life know he has a significant other. No, he's not going to advertise that he has a girlfriend on the first date, and maybe not even on the third or fourth, but when he is ready to claim you as his, he will give you a title both verbally and with his body language. When you walk into a room with him he might put his hand on your waist or maybe he finds a reason to brush your hair back. Whatever way he does it, he subconsciously is sending out a vibe that you are his girl and you are taken, so keep on moving fellas! Sounds very primal, doesn't it ladies? Remember those paragraphs about the male brain? He's predestined to detect challenges of males and he wants to make sure those other men know you are his! Don't let this kind of behavior offend you if it is reasonable (more on that later), let it flatter you. If your man is truly yours he will think you are gorgeous and he won't want to let you go. Accept it, enjoy it, and relish in it!

Heart and brain together

Your Neanderthal will also want to provide for you. Again, it sounds primal, but it's based on basic needs. Sure he might not be able to buy you everything you want, or the most magnificent of things, but that isn't what this is about. He wants to care for you, and again you need to turn loose and let him do that for you. Let me give you an example of this, one of the Neanderthals I know works overtime every week because his wife wanted to be able to stay home with their children. Does he provide her with everything she wants? No, but he was able to give her what she wanted the most and what they need. He might not be able to buy you a new laptop when your old one dies, but he will darn well work his tail off finding a way to get someone to fix it for you!

This protection instinct is both heart and brain working together. He will never in a million years allow anyone to hurt you physically, emotionally, or mentally. This gets weird when the male is too much Neanderthal, and overprotects you to the point of doing all of the things he would never let anyone else do. Again, it's the brain, and possibly heart, working as a cohesive animal instinct to protect what is "his property". The good part of this animalistic structure reminds me of all of those scenes in old Westerns when the good guy gets into a bar fight because he's protecting his lady. By the way, I truly believe we need more men like the ones in Westerns these days... If your man is a true Neanderthal he won't be able to tolerate the thought of you be being in danger from others, himself, or yourself.[15] Obviously, you can visualize what protecting you from others looks like, so let me go a little more in depth on protection from him and yourself.

When I say he will protect you from himself, in no way do I mean he is a danger to you. In fact, if you are reading this and your man is physically, verbally, or emotionally abusive towards you put this book down right now and get help. Any male that intentionally hurts his significant other is nothing but a slimy piece of scum that I wouldn't even bother scraping off of the bottom of my shoe. Period, end of conversation nothing more to be said there.

Moving on... when a man is protecting you from himself it manifests as him withdrawing into himself because he senses that you can't tolerate him being himself. If you have reached this point in your relationship, two things need to happen. First, you need to be willing to let your man express himself. In a more vulgar way, you need to let him have his balls back. A man should be the head of his household and be the one making serious decisions **WITH** you. He is an adult who makes his own decisions and is capable of functioning independently.

---

[15]   (Malinak)

You are not his mother, and he should be a grown man; if he isn't capable of doing so, he is too much of a knuckle-dragging caveman. Second, you need to not only allow him to have "permission" to be himself you need to embrace that, and know that you now have time for your own interests. For example, I hate to fish but it's my Neanderthal's favorite hobby. When we were first married, I thought I had to share that hobby with him and I was miserable! Over time we learned that there was no reason for that and now he does his thing and I stay home and do mine on those nights.

As far as protecting you from yourself, it will absolutely drive a Neanderthal crazy when you make choices that he thinks are illogical, irrational, or outright dangerous to yourself. He knows that you don't think like he does (and if he doesn't, have him read this!). Sometimes, as women, our emotions and hormones get the better of us and we make irrational decisions. He still wants to encompass those issues and make them go away, but we all know that doesn't happen. I am sure many of you have found yourself in the following situation: you and your Neanderthal get into an argument, and you storm out of the house, get in the car, and squeal the tires as you are leaving. You have left your phone, wallet, purse, everything but yourself, your keys, and your car in your fury. Your man is left standing there dumbfounded, without you, his woman; and he realizes he has no way of contacting you, knowing where you are going, or when you will return. He starts to think of you as a child, and begins to treat you in this way because of course, this is how you reacted; but in his mind he is really trying to be your protector, even if he is the one in the wrong. I can't count the number of times I've been in this very same situation, myself.

Neanderthal: "Why would you just drive off without your phone?"

Mind Shaper: "Because sometimes I just need to clear my head, much like you guys do. It's only frowned upon when we females do it!"

Neanderthal: "But how are we supposed to protect you if you leave?"

Mind Shaper: "Good question, it's the one time we don't think about anything in that moment…"

Neanderthal: "But seconds later, you're thinking about everything else again!"

Mind Shaper: "It's our one moment when we can actually be like you men with a one-directional operative, only yours is during sex!"

The Neanderthal, when protecting you from yourself, even reacts to you picking yourself apart; reminding you that he revels in your hips or whatever body part you are angry at for that moment. To the Neanderthal, it does not matter about your tiny scars. He sees the whole picture, and this is what is relevant to him. He truly is attracted to you, and is trying to protect you from your own words. At these moments, it can be hard to remember that your Neanderthal only wants to protect you; from not only the world around you, but your own self defecating opinions about what you do not see as good in yourself. The true Neanderthal will notice the small things, but will not nit-pick them as much as you will, because each person is their own enemy when it comes to matters of one's own heart.

Let it be heart or brain, men and women are very different when it comes to showing affection to one another; but when a man sets his sights on capturing "the one," mating with her becomes his prime directive. When he succeeds, his brain makes an indelible imprint of her. Lust and devotion collide and he's hooked.[16] <3 vs. lust is a whole other ball of wax, combined in the heart and brain which will be circled to later (we wouldn't want our Neanderthal writer to not have an opinion on that) It is an important distinction that both sexes have different wiring, which effects the way we amore each other and the beings around us.

---

[16]   (Brizendine, 2010)

Neandergirl

a compassionate soul

A child knows compassion and pain, but not in the essence that an adult does. Children hold strong feelings of unconditional emotions towards others, sometimes better than what most adults do. This next story is about a little Neandergirl and her endearment for what moved her forward in life. At a very young age, she was compelled to take in stray animals. Her mother passed away during her birth, and her father worked all the time, so she was raised by her aunt and uncle who lived on four acres of open land. At age eight, she was playing in the yard when she saw a kitten with a bum leg, asked her auntie if she could help it and of course the answer was yes. After nursing the kitten to good health she had this new look about her, almost an elated glow, that every time she was near the cat her smile got bigger, and little did she know her happy receptors in her brain were overloaded. The girl gave the little furry ball a name, *Tinks*, a chance to live, and of course a family and home. For the girl she was considered to have fallen head over heels with something that made her life better.

The little girl grew up with Tinks, but managed to accommodate about 9 other species as well before attending high school. From skunks to horses she had a gamut of animals. Her aunt and uncle helped teach her about the animals as she became enthusiastic about helping the animals almost as much as her own passion for her endeared Tinks. The girl, through high school and then into college, never yearned for the feeling of someone as companionship, because she focused all of her efforts on being the best veterinarian she could be. She dated a few people, but did not seek out to feel smitten with anyone who did not admire her animals as much as she did. She sought work over suitors, and gave all of her heart towards saving as many animals as possible.

Tinks had passed away her last year of college before she became a vet assistant. The cat passed from old age, but the Nearndergirl could not part with her best friend so easily. The girl, now a young woman, decided to keep her pet as a stuffed creature curled into a ball the way it passed so that she could take her friend with her and keep her passions for her work astride; knowing that her best friend could be with her no matter where she went. Yes, a little creepy, but it was the only thing that gave her that feeling or emotion which most share with someone else.

Neanderthal: "Wait a minute, you mean to tell me you can brazen your emotions to an object or animal as much as a human?"

Mind Shaper: "Yes, some people have stronger compassions or connections towards objects than they do people!"

Neanderthal: "That's just weird!"

Mind Shaper: "Don't worry; it's just another layer of this impeccable word! Now, stop interrupting so we can get back to the story."

The Neanderwoman nearly around her mid-forties had accomplished many things; such as becoming a business owner for a prestigious vet clinic, owned many animals on her acreage, and even had the chance to travel the world doing the thing she enjoyed the most. The one thing she felt a little perturbed about was that the suitors that were around weren't quite up to her expectations or high standards, which she valued for herself, but she had decided on giving one a chance. The male, whom she thought would be a good fit had actually been in her life for many years off and on again; and definitely didn't care that some saw her as the animal lady.

The male grew up a town away, was five years her elder, and had helped a few times with a couple of animals when they were younger. They actually attended the same high school for a year. The male applied for the Neandergirls' future college, but chose a different one so he could pursue being a doctor. After all his work and strides in life he decided to move to a small town to start his own pediatric center. Funny thing though, the now Neanderwoman had actually opened her own vet clinic in the same small town that the Doctor was in. He had been married once before and had a child with a lady whom he thought was the one, but turned out not to be. After nearly twelve years, the two divorced and had joint custody of their child. A few years after the divorce, he brought in a stray dog that had been involved in an accident, almost like the movie, *"Turner and Hooch,"* only the dog was not as big and messy and the man was not Tom Hanks. The dog healed nicely and became the man's best friend. There was a wondrous magic that came over the two of them whilst talking about making sure the dog would be okay. The male asked the vet if she would like to get coffee one morning. Afterwards, these two were inseparable when they were not working, and could be seen holding hands in the park or just walking around town. Whether due to proximity, timing, or whatever, after about five years of dating the male asked the vet if she would like to engage in life as his partner. She said yes, as long as she could keep her separate house so she had a place to escape, and somewhere for her items related to her work to go. He agreed and stated that would make things easier, if anything, because they were so used to being independent for so long, that neither should give up too much of themselves just to make the other happy; but they knew that the other one held that special thing they had been searching for within a mate.

They lived in separate houses for nearly a decade after they got married, putting them in their 60's, but spent evenings together; trading weeks in different houses, and opposite for the weekends. They even spent one day a week where they didn't see each other on purpose, when work did not get in the way. The two eventually moved in together around the time that he retired, sold one house and both had sold their businesses. The two grew very old together and had combined themselves in every aspect. One evening while the male was arranging the closet looking for something, he found a very interesting box that he had never noticed before. The box was decorated and was very ornate with ribbons and bows. He pulled it out and took a peek inside only to see the first thing the Neanderwoman actually felt she would be lost if she didn't have, her cat, *Tinks.* Confused, he asked his dearest what this was and why she had it. Her response was, "I have extreme feelings for you, but if my cat couldn't have been with me or can't be here now, then I don't want to be." The male snickered but looked at her with astonishment and made one comment, "If this is the craziest thing that you have had to keep from me, then it must be something precious, much like our time we have together." A few months later the vet passed away in her sleep and her only request was that she be laid with her secret box and eventually one day next to her best man.

The male respected her wishes with the secret box, and visited her site everyday when the two would normally go for a walk. Two years, to the day, the male followed in her steps and joined her side in the earth and unto the other side. As they lay before the land the headstone just above the date stated, "A beautiful woman, her first love, *Tinks,* and the man who embraced them both."

Neanderlating

connecting with others

"Ung grunt ror nonk drrr ooooot nict buun tchu sssooo?" Or translated, as there are so many ways to mention infatuation and how we relate it to others and objects. To our Neanderthal, he is now close to ready to show compassion in many ways, but now as he prepares to utilize these items, the challenge is how to relate them. Life experiences have allowed us to come to the understanding that men relate to others differently than women do. Men shape relationships, friendships and romances, through shared activities and interest. A woman's connection, whether it be with male or female, are wired to bond deeper than just activities and interest. From a smile to the characteristics of our eyes, women bond in essence almost on a sub-conscious level that is hard to explain. Shared interests do make for a stronger bond, so it is important to share hobbies with your Neanderthal, and let him share in your interests as well; even if it takes time and compromise for both of you to find common ground. If you can't find common hobbies, then you should probably reevaluate your relationship and yourselves; making time to spend together in an activity you both enjoy and that will help your personal attachment. Plus, you might find something you really enjoy that you never imagined would be awesome.

Now, this doesn't mean you have to engage in hobbies or activities you hate or despise, but you should show some genuine interest in the items you don't share. For example, if your Neanderthal, or if your modern day man, is interested in fantasy football and you don't care about it in the least, you should take a little time to create a basic understanding about this subject, so you can actively engage in conversation about it. Fellas' this goes for you as well, but remember you do not need to know every shoe brand or the most up to date problems in the magazines, just show some attention where it is due. I cannot count how many hours I've spent in fishing supply stores bored out of my mind. By being there or asking him how his fishing trip was (and then listening to a 20 minute description of the fish that he caught or missed), I let him know I was genuinely interested in him, and helped give us a better relationship. It's the same for him when he goes shopping with me, even though he really doesn't want to. He is actively participating with what makes me happy.

Neanderthal: "I have gone to museums, went shopping and learned new skills with my ladies and had a great time!"

Mind Shaper: "That's good Neanderthal, you're on the right path to learning how to communicate with that special someone. All you have to do now is get it down to ONE lady!"

Neanderthal: "That sounds way difficult."

Mind Shaper: "Really? Because if you have only one person to worry about, you don't have to deal with the drama of everyone else!"

Neanderthal men or women interact with a different type of passion towards their acquaintances and true friends. For men, they typically have fewer true close friendships, but they have larger networks of associates and other connections. Women are more apt to have many friends but a smaller network, unless they are atop of an empire that they created. It's also interesting to view how Neanderthals interact when they are upset with their true compassionate friends. It is a completely different emotional tie than that of two beings whom are captivated by each other. A more encompassing connection happens with buddies or amigos; and can be perceived as a brotherhood/sisterhood that looks stronger than an intimate bond we create within our mates.

Certain squabbles and arguments with males and females almost always tend to be stereotypical. Females tend to be catty, focus on gossipy bull shit, and hold a grudge over a tiny problem even if they have been friends for years. Their true loyalty will remain with their chosen suitor and themselves, even if that means ending friendships that are decades long. While males try duking it out verbally, physically and loudly showing an assertive dominance; then clanking beers together as soon as the disagreement is over, moving on with life, and continuing to remain friends. Neanderthal men have a certain loyalty to their clan or tribe; however, once you break the confidence or trust of this man you are very unlikely to ever regain it.

Neanderthal: "So if I upset a woman for a minute, she's going to hold it against me for a year?"

Mind Shaper: "Probably, but you may hold a grudge against her during an argument as well, just not for as long."

From a female's perspective, the country song, "Find Out Who Your Friends Are," by Tracy Lawrence is a perfect example of this:

> You find out who your friends are
>
> Somebody's gonna drop everything
>
> Run out and crank up their car
>
> Hit the gas get there fast
>
> Never stop to think 'what's in it for me?' or 'it's way too far.'
>
> They just show on up with their big old heart

You find out who you're friends are[17]

One non-barbaric way that men connect with others, or cope with stress, is to try to diffuse the tension with humor. I know personally this can infuriate me as a woman if I'm already annoyed, but the humor is usually with good intent. Ladies, you might as well learn to laugh at your Neanderthal's ridiculous jokes and other nonsense, or you're going to have a long and miserable time in your relationship. Being able to enjoy each other's company, have fun, and laugh together is an essential part of a long-term commitment.

In connection to how we relate with each other, let's talk about a basic difference with how men and women communicate. It has been researched and proven that women feel more connected when they talk to their partner face to face, whereas men often feel close when they work, play or talk side by side.[18] Psychiatrist Alfred Scheflen studied this concept and categorized the way we sense our own personal space into what he called "frames." He believed that when people talk their shoulder orientation adjusts. [19]

---

[17] (Beathard & Hill, 2006)

[18] (Cohen, 2007)

[19] (Nelson, 2014)

Generally, when women talk to each other or men we turn our shoulders towards each other and typically maintain eye contact. We also tend to lean forward, nod our heads, smile and touch more while conversing. This allows us to focus on the other person's face, create a bond through eye contact, keep the person we are talking with engaged and read emotions. However, when men talk side by side they don't necessarily look at each other, because again, in the animal world face to face eye contact can be a sign of dominance or competition. They also are not as interested at looking face to face or keeping eye contact because it is sometimes considered confrontational to them from an instinctive point. Men do not usually tend to read facial emotions subconsciously like women typically do. So how do a man and woman orientate themselves to talk to each other comfortably? Helen Fisher said it best, "A woman should probably adopt at least one nonverbal, side-by-side leisure activity that her spouse enjoys, whereas men could improve their home lives if they took time out to sit face to face with their mates to engage in talk and active listening."[20] Genius!

---

[20]   (Fisher, 1994)

So as both sexes try to take on subtle changes to grow and initiate that compassionate bond, we learn that with brain, heart, communication, body language, experiences and primal instincts we can start to actually fall for each other. As we fall, we learn that visually we are attracted to certain attributes; but really do not become enamored with each other just by viewing them, unless by a lustful infatuation. Now let us (you the reader, myself and the Neanderthal) try and divulge a bit more unto the relationship status quo and figure out whether it is falling in complete inoculation with someone or if it is a mere flirtatious embodiment of lust.

Before You Can Fall

As cliché as it is, you have to learn to be comfortable with yourself before you can truly indulge in another. Unlike my previous writing, most of the things I am listing here are what I've learned from my own experiences, not backed by research or science; so take them as you will. I recommend you check out the wonderful writing of Addie Zierman's post, "For the One Who Married Young," on her blog "How to Talk Evangelical."[21]

---

[21]   (Zierman, 2013)

She is writing for a Christian audience who married young, but many of her thoughts resonate with my own.

You have to know who you are and what makes yourself tick before allowing someone in. The challenge is finding what works within the relationships you hold while striving to move towards creating a long lasting bond. Sometimes, we put work or life in front of these, but instinctually we thrive to find one that complements our life.

First, you must create your own independence. You are building a relationship with another person but you cannot lose your inner self. Remember that you were single once before, what did you do in your spare time that you enjoyed? Did you love to play a sport, knit, travel? Make sure you keep doing what you enjoy! A relationship is two people who have joined together in a commitment; but that doesn't mean you are one entity, you are still your half of this relationship. Sadly, no relationship lasts forever, but the bonds created within will always be memories. At some point in your lives you will separate, either because mutual separation or death of your other half. You need to retain some of yourself so you know who to be when that time comes. If you are lucky enough to be enamored with your significant other all the way through marriage and then death, you may be alone if they pass before you; and you will want some piece of you still alive even if you feel you can't live without them, because that part of you is the part that you fell for within yourself. Those that date and separate, or marry and divorce, find themselves a few times; but they also find that spark or interest within others at different times in their lives. Both situations have perks and disillusions of what true adoration is, neither is completely right or wrong; it is upon each individual situation and how your relationships are built.

To really be with someone else you have to know yourself first. Are you an introvert or extravert, type A or type B, etc.? Do you enjoy your own personal space and time? You need to figure yourself out first, then you can better relate to your Neanderthal man or woman. Try to see what types they are (it might be a cool conversational piece). For example, I am an introvert and I need me time to recharge when I'm socially exhausted and it took me years to really figure that out. Until I took time to reflect on that, my poor Neanderthal got the brunt of my, "I'm emotionally drained and exhausted, don't even look at me for now!" irritation. However, once I started figuring out myself and could explain it to him, we quickly found a solution that works for both of us.

In addition, it is essential that you are willing to compromise; don't be selfish because that will not work for either of you. You have to be able to give in and come up with mutually agreeable solutions to the problems that will arise in your relationship. Sometimes, that means neither of you is really happy, but can tolerate whatever life is throwing at you in that moment. Sometimes, it can mean one person will be happy and the other will just have to live with it, but hopefully only for a short while. When it's time to compromise, the best solution is to communicate calmly and rationally; to find out if the item or situation is really important, and how two beings come to the outcome even if they aren't enthusiastic about it. You have to be willing to let loose some of the things for the greater good.

Can you accept who your man is or is he going to have to change for you? Neither of you should have to compromise who you are, but be willing to accept changes that will happen over time. Yes, he's going to have quirks that drive you insane, I promise; however, ladies you cannot change who a man is on the inside. Hell, your quirks are going to make him wonder what makes you tick and why you do what you do as you explore life together. You might be able to modify little things, but to truly be devoted to someone you have to be willing to accept who they are inside and out. If the list of things you want to change about your partner is long and full of major personality traits, either the two of you are not a match for each other or you are not ready for this relationship. Over time if you try to spend too much time changing your significant other into something they are not, it changes them from your first initial intrigue. Think about it for yourself, as the reader; would you want to be in a relationship with someone who constantly tried to make you into something you're not? Doubtful.

I'm not saying you and your relationship won't change over time, but what you will do is grow together or apart. I love how Addie Zierman says it, "When you marry young, you'll change and he'll change, and in the midst of all of this growth you'll realize that you can't change each other. There will be moments and days and seasons that are *really hard.* And you'll be tempted to think it's because you *got married young,* but really, it's just because you got married.[22]" Even though she's referencing young marriages, this is true for all relationships.

I can sum up all I've said in this section with this list of questions... think hard about each, and answer each one

---

[22] (Zierman, 2013)

honestly. If you can answer each of these affirmatively, you are in what I believe is a mature, passionate relationship.

Are you willing to?
<ul><li>Give unconditional, selfless, serving adoration to someone else</li><li>Give everything you have of yourself for the other's benefit</li><li>Give all you have physically, mentally, emotionally, spiritually, for your significant other, even when you don't feel like it</li><li>Put his/her needs above your own no matter how you feel</li><li>Be his/her biggest fan</li><li>Have his/her back even when you disagree</li><li>Never compromise his/her character or confidences in front of others</li><li>Be best friends</li><li>Keep trying even when it gets hard</li><li>Compromise for his/her better good</li><li>Make an effort to show how much you care for each other every day!</li></ul>

That is an attention-grabbing list. If these questions were hard to answer, you are not ready for a long-lasting relationship, but rather something short-term, which is okay. Sometimes, we have to go through many short-term relationships in order to find the one truly meaningful relationship that will be built to last.

Neanderthal: "So what you're saying, is it's okay to play the field?"

Mind Shaper: "It's not always the best thing, but some people tend to find it by way of trial and error."

Neanderthal: "So what else could be missing?"

Mind Shaper: "Nothing is really missing, but the connection between people is much stronger when they start out as friends first."

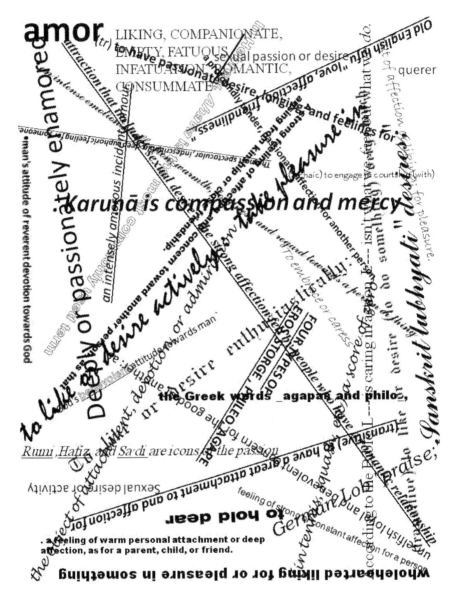

amor (tr) to LIKING, COMPANIONATE, EMPTY, FATUOUS, INFATUATION, ROMANTIC, CONSUMMATE sexual passion or desire

passionately enamored

to like or passionately

Karuṇā is compassion and mercy

Desire actively

Deeply

the Greek words _agapaŋ and philo_,

Rumi, Hafiz, and Sa'di are icons for the passion

Sexual desire for activity

. a feeling of warm personal attachment or deep affection, as for a parent, child, or friend.

to hold dear

Wholehearted liking for or pleasure in something

old English querer

Sanskrit lubhyati "desires"

"No matter where or who, there is always another way to interpret this word"

Neanderboned

the other connection

Neanderthal: "What's this title? Are we getting food?"

Mind Shaper: "In essence. It's time to mention another type of hunger."

Neanderthal: "So we're not having turkey legs?"

Mind Shaper: "No, something more fantastic!"

So, we've slightly talked about the brain, the heart, how we fall, what the feelings are, and even the confusion of what it all means. Now, let's discuss the part no one wants to talk about, but helps create the most sensitive bond; because every neuron, every inch of skin, most brain waves, and even thoughts are escalated and heightened, sometimes as a lustful adventure and other times as another awesome energy of pure devotion.

Think about a typical male/female relationship and how it is formed. Within men, testosterone takes over while they seek to find the person they want to choose as their "one", their "trophy", "the old lady" per say, which changes a boy from a seed spreading adolescent to the man and father he can become. This special lady is the one that the Neanderthal decides to protect, care for and lives life with. Even though there may be multiple people in the Neanderthal's clan, he is devoted to this specific one, no matter what. Sometimes, those chauvinistic pigs of men are just trying to spread seed and never actually know a stronger emotion other than that of lust. Instinctively, it is not emotion they are thinking with, but rather a feeling of body and exploration than a feeling of devotion. More than likely, these men are trying to fill a void within themselves, and the best way for them to do that is through sex because they have not yet found or felt what the meaning or understanding of the higher more powerful emotion. If they have found this meaning, they still may just want sex, which also is okay because it is human nature. Though women are called sluts in this same endeavor when they sleep around trying to get the right "fit" (pun maybe intended) so that as they grow a life together with a male; he is deemed the best for her and her dreams, and perhaps will become her knight in shining armor. Men don't think that way on the outside, but deep down the men that play the field are sluts as well, because hell, they are trying to find the right "spoon" or companion who encourages them to want to be a better man. Not everyone follows this same path of what could be construed as weakness because on the other end of the scale, sex is power. It can lead into happiness, and sometimes true fondness. Both parties, male and female, are looking for that dominance, the protector, the one who brings out the best and worst, whether within themselves or in chances of trying to grow a family.

Let it be lust, sex, excitement, a challenge, or more, it is a start of infatuation that blooms into confidence in all parties, building a small tier of true companionship; though it rarely is more than maybe a few one night stands or very short term relationships. Our Modern Day Neanderthal may only know the feeling in his loins (the most primitive instinct), but for you the reader, we can take a situation and decide if in our lives it is more of a romantic gesture or fun flirtations. Generally, but not always, men explore earlier than woman do; but later in life woman tend to be on the prowl searching for that intimate connection more than men do in their teenage years, thus creating our "cougars" and "cubs" in today's society. True fervor could last a long time, but only as long as we accept it, no matter what the age range is. In reality, we all know that certain desires can and will be short and quick, and are supposed to be fun, but might not mean anything at all. Many people whom are enamored with their mate forget that they too can still have those feelings of thirst for each other, but it will take communication and some compromises. Singles who mingle know that there is no compromise within themselves, other than the fact that they may make a bad decision or end up having the best time of their life. Whereas with couples tend to feel that they have to compromise and schedule intimate time, spontaneity becomes a lost thought sometimes when in a long term relationship. This is when we choose what meaning, symbols and ideals we want to associate and attach to these amorous feelings we have. We know some of the consequences of both ends if we say that word to the mate of the night or the long term companion.

Perhaps a comparison of the two, lust and <3, are what can help you understand that both are important. First, let me explain to you my feeling on this situation. Often people who are in what I'll call "young relationships[23]" will proclaim to the world that they are in <3. However, their relationship has not matured enough for them to truly be in <3, what they are typically experiencing is what I call being in lust. Over time, and with work, lust can turn into a more meaningful relationship, but it takes work and commitment to do so. A quick Google search will give you thousands of links to articles, quizzes, and other pages about being in <3 vs. lust. So let's use that 21st century

---

[23] A "young relationship" is not determined by the length of the relationship but by its maturity. See "Before You Can <3" section for more information.

resource to set some basic parameters. Below is a small chart that shows the two sides of what we are exploring.

Lust	<3
• Focus on physical attraction	• Affection, not just attraction
• Sex, not conversation and connection	• Desire to spend time together
• The "Charlie Harper" Effect ○ Leave right after sex	• Willing to compromise • Desire for long term commitment to each other
• No deep conversations about feelings	
• Short term enjoyment	
• Only pleasure seeking	
• No or only temporary commitment	

The chart seems to make the representation of the two different perceptions of what this word is to some people simple and easy. For singles the lust side = sex which is actually simple for them, but by way of the brain it is convoluted and complicated. It becomes more layers of what compassion is, and yes, there are people that truly only are in amore with sex and not the people at hand; again, another way which that one word has a different meaning and feeling attached. The thing about sex is that each performance, while different from the others or latest, are similar, but different, even with the same person. Whether in a relationship for six months or 50 or more years, is not a single act that is the same everytime. It is that desire that builds on the sex the night before, the year before, the decade before. Sex is a matter that unfolds like an accordion in the brain, the past is connected to the near past, the near past to the present, and the present to the future, which stands there waiting to be attached to the next event. When people state that they're "sex life" has changed or is non-existent, it is because the files in their brain remind them that it was something that had a connection with someone who created emotional ties. So the feelings in the body, the feelings for someone else, the excitement of the new, or the welcome of the familiar rises and falls, depends on memory, gains its depth from what happened at the beginning, a while ago, in the imagination, and in reality.[24]

Even though you think it is simple, sex is probably the most misunderstood topic between a Neanderthal man and his woman, so I couldn't finish my sections of this without talking about it and clearing up some things for both sexes. So, what do women really need to know about sex when it comes to

---

[24]   (...., 2011)

their Neanderthal man? Mostly things that seem like common sense, at least to them...

Neanderthal: "Really? We're pretty simple..."

Mind Shaper: "Then tell me, what do we ladies need to know about Neanderthal men and sex???"

Neanderthal: "To the female - no play, no flirt, just straight to the point, stop mixin signals...no excuses all the time. All we want to do is just have some fun!"

Mind Shaper: "For you males, try to romance it up a bit - don't always hit it in a minute to quit it, sometimes just listen to us!"

Neanderthal: "Sometimes we are not thinking, we just want sex. Other times we just want to be left alone."

Mind Shaper: "And you talk about US mixing up our signals?"

Neanderthal: "If you just focus on the act, in the moment, and stop over thinking it, and everything else, we wouldn't have such a problem."

Mind Shaper: "Ugh, stupid men, don't you know we have to think about the laundry, the bills, is my hair too tight, are my boobs okay, is my vagina nice, will it be okay if I fart..."

Neanderthal: "Okay...ENOUGH! Let's get back to the story, my brain hurts now!"

Mind Shaper: "Mine too! Oh yeah, I forgot the groceries!"

First and foremost, take into consideration what you know from personal experiences or have already read about how your man's brain works and how he relates with you. All of that still applies when sex is involved; in fact, I'd say that sex underlies most of what has already been established. It's important to understand that a majority of men are highly sexual creatures, with a very high drive and are extremely motivated by sex.

Mind Shaper: "Which means with the right motivation I can get my car washed, haha!"

Neanderthal: "Yeah, but you women are sex-pots, too. Don't act all innocent! I mean most of the time, all you do is tease us!

Mind Shaper: "Well, if you weren't so focused on your video games, mechanics, and fantasy leagues, I wouldn't have to use MY red room fantasies just to get your attention!"

Neanderthal: "Oh really...?"

Mind Shaper: "In all due seriousness, it's important to understand what motivates anyone, especially your partner."

Let's start with communication styles. Remember that the Neander-man is very direct and straightforward. They don't do well with subtle hints and clues; being flirtatious is always fun, but sometimes it can be a challenge for them to decode those mysterious lady signals. For example, you might spend a lot of time getting ready to go out on a date, making sure you look smoking hot, but have no intention of anything beyond flirtation. However, in reality, for him his switch is either off or on, and there's no in between; and to be honest 90% of the time his switch is probably on. This is why so many men get in trouble with the cliché, "I just want a backrub." I'm not implying that consent is irrelevant, what I am saying is that you should be very clear with your intentions. If your ending goal is that you want sex, just tell him. In his mind, that's a win and you don't even have to try; just say the word "**SEX**" and watch him react. If sex is not on the table, then be more upfront about it, because what your small, subtle flirtations may be to you, are dangerous to him because he is ready to pounce on you because you are his prey for that moment. He may be disappointed, but he will respect your honesty. Just know, you ladies cannot automatically assume sex is the only thing on his mind, and you must respect him if he says that's not what he wants at that time. I'm stating these ideals from being a very happily married woman, and I've learned these things by the communication I share with my significant other. As for the Neanderthal, we may be good friends, but I have witnessed some of these very instances in his single life at attempting to find compassion from a potential mate.

In researching for this book, there were many late night conversations with both married couples and single people. One of the most enlightening moments for both the men and women in the room involved a conversation about what we women see in ourselves versus what the men looking at us see. With a few tears, one of the women disclosed that she is self-conscious about her breasts because she thinks they are saggy and uneven. Being the good friends they are the guys laughed and told her that any Neander-man would be oblivious to the sag or uneven-ness, but instead would be thrilled to be looking at breasts.

Now, let's talk about how our female brain works. Often, females are very concerned with the million things that they see as wrong with their bodies. We see every stretch mark, bump, and stray hair; we're concerned about the size of our butt and think about how we look constantly. A true Neanderthal man is not interested in any of those things that we see wrong in ourselves. When your clothes come off instead of seeing all of those faults, he sees fun, excitement, danger, SEX! He sees a naked woman, his prize, his accomplishment, and imagines everything he can do to you in a split second! As he goes to act upon his animalistic needs, all he thinks about is sex (and sometimes baseball just to make it last a little longer).

Spending so much time being concerned about our own looks, makes us self-conscious and we start to doubt ourselves; and unfortunately can't see the person that our partner sees at that particular moment.

Sometimes, men don't understand that for women sex can be a very mental experience, often hindered by our own perceived faults. Many times, we are so caught up in how we look, the bills on the counter, and the laundry on the floor that we allow our minds to wander with minor concerns, making it difficult to put all of our thoughts into the experience of romance, or just sex. Unfortunately, because so much of a woman's sexual enjoyment is affected by mental focus and emotional connection, without a clear understanding and patience it can be difficult for two people to create a genuine connection that extends beyond the bedroom.

This also means that it's important for all parties involved to understand that sometimes our female brains just are not on the same wavelength as theirs (this relates to all sexual experiences including singles, married couples, same sex partners, or people involved in any other encounters). I could have countless things running through my mind which would make it almost impossible to enjoy sex.

One of the best parts of being with a Neanderthal man is that he is interested in more than just pleasure for himself, and he takes great pride and joy in being able to provide *enjoyment* for his partner. This is where that straightforward method of communication becomes very important. It's important for both partners to be clear in what brings them enjoyment and what each one desires.

Along those lines, because they are such a high drive creature, Neander-men often seem to have a sexual bucket list or a checklist in their mind that I imagine is similar to unlocking video game achievements (remember, they think you are their trophy). Each achievement is like a bonus round, a one upper on their friends, something they can brag about, "like sticking it in the pooper," or finding out if she has a gag reflex or not. Whether they are monogamous or with multiple partners, they are constantly searching for something new and fun to try. In retrospect, we women have our own checklist of achievements, which include getting our man to dress up in a suit, nice dinners, romantic walks, flowers, encompassing each others' bodies slowly instead of just bumping and grinding, or someone just being manly around the house. Either way, we each have our own goals, which fit with our way of thinking, but it all seems to come with the price of sex or sexual favors. These can lead to a more passionate connection, but often times it's just sex.

It's interesting to see that Neander-men approach the world through a straightforward and highly sexually motivated way. Single Neander-men often spend a majority of time in pursuit of new sexual adventures and encounters, whereas a monogamous Neander-man tends to approach the world with just his highly sexual drive, which is focused on his partner. This focus enables them to set goals for a bucket list, as well as look for new adventures. I guarantee you if you were to ask your partner, in a non-confrontational way, if they have any sexual desires they would like to try, they would be able to list at least a couple things they would like to experience. The main thing is to keep those lines of communication open and safe. Not only will it help build your relationship, but it will make it a whole lot more fun along the way.

Sex for both women and men is an experience and not just saying that four letter word to get into someone's pants. Yes that happens but because at that time the word gets misconstrued and is probably true in the heat of the moment. Whether sex is good, bad, intrigued with mystery, or just plain ole intrinsic for reproduction, it is the one sentiment that gets confused with what amore is. The two items are very different; though one can enjoy having them individually or all encompassing. Each person will relate that passion of having another person to themselves in the way they feel necessary; let it be for fun or for true endearment but that is for you to decide within that exact moment.

Neanderthal: "So if sex is involved then it could be a wild rollercoaster of amore, but with lots of distractions"

Mind Shaper: "Yes! All the emotions, feelings, and distractions are the rollercoaster, sex is just a hill, amore is the whole ride"

Neanderthal: "Oh so no sex no passion"?

Mind Shaper: "Sometimes sex has to be out of the equation and that passion is just as strong if not stronger in some instances of true adoration"

Neandertime

short time long time

The First Entry

The doctors suggested that I start writing to channel my thoughts and emotions in this Journal. I think they believe it will help them understand what is going on in my head, and that they will learn something new from this. It helps me sleep sometimes as I use it to get rid of the pain inside, which will never really go away. The other inmates, patients, whatever you call us here, are afraid of me because they think I'm crazy. I know I'm not, but I'm pretty sure they are. It works out best that way; I get to spend most of my time by myself in the few hours a week they let us out to "socialize."

I have told my story a thousand times, and each and every time it has been the same; and no matter how much I "channel my thoughts and emotions" the story is not going to change because it is the truth. I think this would all have been a lot simpler if I would have lied; but my parents raised me to never lie, and never steal; and no matter what anyone thinks my conscious and morality haven't changed from this.

I am so tired of being here, I would give anything to go home to my family, my husband, my dogs, my friends but I will not lie and I know they will never let me leave. Even if I was to go home, I doubt that anyone but my dogs would take me back. At night I dream of going home and finding my family and friends laughing and talking around a hot meal, and when they see me enter they gasp, stare, and then scream and run from me. I run after them calling to them until I spot myself in reflections and see myself as a terrifying monster. The doctors say this is a manifestation of my internal guilt, and I think that is bullshit. The truth is so much simpler and I could have found it without the hours of "psychoanalysis" and "therapy." It is not my guilt that is manifested in these dreams that wake me up screaming and crying every night, but the fear and disdain that my endeared ones feel towards me. They don't see me as myself any longer but as a monster that is to be feared and ashamed of.

When this first started my mother and father would visit me and beg me to, "tell them what really happened," even though they have heard the same story over and over. They would cry and tell me they raised me better than this and then it turned into anger and horror at how I could do this to them. Eventually, they stopped coming to see me; I think they wish I would just disappear. Joe visits me when they allow him to but his eyes are empty when he looks at me. I have told him I'm sorry for what happened but he doesn't understand how I say this, but not regret what I've done.

It's late and I'm exhausted but that's nothing new, I've been exhausted for months. Every night the dreams come, I dread lying down because every time I close my eyes I see it again; and if I'm lucky I eventually drift off but then dream of it, or my monster-self. I have to lie down; I can't keep my eyes open any longer.

September...sometime

I lay in bed as long as I could stand. I think I must have slept for an hour and a half total between the dreams and images that dance on the back of my eyelids. Tonight was no different than any of the other nights; I couldn't stop seeing things that have already happened. I kept seeing Joe's face from months ago; it was the last time I remember seeing him cry. His face was wet and he begged me to forgive him when he passed the divorce papers to me.

It was like I was floating above the glass wall between us, I could see his hands shaking as he wept and begged me to sign them. I could almost see the look of betrayal in my eyes and then hear myself screaming, but I was so much more than screams inside me. I remember sitting there feeling a huge lump gathering in my throat; I could hear the begging and pleading in my mind, but the lump in my throat choked out my words and all I could do was scream. Of course, the guards were ready because I am sure they knew this was coming; why else would they have a sedative ready for me? I'm watching from above again when I see one of the guards slip a syringe from his shirt pocket as he and the other five burly and cold men move towards me. I continue to scream as the first two grab my arms and then I see Joe's face and the look of pity and sadness in his eyes as he mouths the word, "please." That one sad look and emphatic "please" is on a continuous loop in my mind tonight, hell every night… Maybe I can go back to my holding facility to lie back down for a few minutes; I hope I can sleep a little this week…

Is this Autumn?

I swear, if this journal doesn't kill me, the doctors or my room will. Today I heard them whispering that I had sociopathic tendencies, like I'm Hannibal Lector or some weird specimen to be poked and prodded. When I looked at them, acknowledging that I heard them, they all looked away from me. During my short time I'm allowed to read and research. I looked up what this meant. I can see why they believe it, I guess. They insist that I write the events that lead me here. So yet again, my story remains the same page after page. The doctors suggested that I start writing...

December 6

Joe and Sam were best friends; they met in 5th grade when Joe moved to Buffalo from the Carolina coast. It was just he and his mom, and needless to say it was a big change for Joe. When he and Sam met it was like they'd been friends for their whole lives. Through their school years they were inseparable. They would fight like brothers but end up right back together. Joe spent a lot of time at Sam's with his family and was an unofficial member of the family. Joe and I met in college, and it was clear that if I was going to date Joe I was going to be spending a lot of time with Sam, too. Over time, I not only had a romantic relationship with Joe, but Sam became like my brother.

Joe and I got through school and moved into a townhouse and when Sam needed a place to stay also, there was no question that he would stay with us. When Joe worked second shift, it was Sam and I. When Sam's girlfriend decided she wanted to sleep around, Joe and I talked to him all night long for days. When Joe and I bickered and argued, Sam would always be there to mediate and help settle everything down. We were a tripod through the good and bad days, sort of inseparable; and that's how this all started.

Sam's ex was seeing someone new and she had told this muscle-head all kinds of lies about Sam, Joe, and me. It started online and over the phone, but escalated to Sam having to file a restraining order against both his ex and her meat-head boyfriend, Zach. It was so bad that Sam could no longer take the train to work, like he had for years, and Joe and I were picking him up and dropping him off on our way into town every day.

I'll never forget the call to Sam on February 21st. I was on my way to pick him up; when I called him to let him know I was coming. He stepped out of his office's lobby and was waiting for me on the street, when he saw that idiot meat-head coming down the street with three of his thuggish friends.

February, one year later

Again I write, but it is still the same, just more pain and anguish every time since I can never be who I was, only what they want me to be in here.

I hear that whispered panicked phone call with Sam day after day, over and over .....

"Ella, it's Sam, Zach is heading towards me up the street. I think he's coming for me...hurry!"

I hit the gas and started honking my horn for people to get out of my way. I hear Sam turn to the person behind him and whisper for them to call 911. I hear a struggle and then hear a woman scream about a knife. I hear Zach that muscle bound piece of shit, growling at Sam and Sam pleading for his life. I don't think I'm ever going to get there. As I turn down the street with what seems like two blocks to go I hear a crash and Sam's phone hits the pavement and he screams. I hear the blood curling scream of a woman, and then realize that scream is me.

Entry

The doctors suggested that I start writing...I miss Joe so much, I wish he knew how much he means to me, even if it is through the glass. He has a fear in his eye, and yet, I know deep down he may be losing the bond we once had...

As I pull up to the curb screaming I see Sam lying on the sidewalk in a pool of his own blood surrounded by shocked coworkers. I see that shit muscle Zach and his idiots running down the street. I don't know what comes over me but I speed up away from Sam. I am yelling, my breath hitching, and I feel tears pouring down my face. As Zach starts to cross the street in front of me, I slam the gas and hear a thump as his body smashes against my windshield. I hit the man that killed my friend. I can still feel the shards and shatters that assaulted me in my car as his body makes the airbag pop and he flips over my car. I slam the car in reverse and hit the gas. THUMP, THUMP. Yes, I ran over him again and no I'm still not sorry. I stop the car, get out, and start to run back to Sam.

May 10

I hope I can sleep a little this week…The doctors suggested I start writing…The image is burned into my brain but I do not know which is worse -- the blood of my dear friend as it pooled near him as I sit with him on the sidewalk, or that I took my own justice without fear because I believed that SOB deserved what he got…

I run back to Sam dodging the cars, passers-by, police, and ambulances and when I get back to Sam and fall on my knees next to him, I hold him and talk to him as he takes his last few breaths. I remember the last words I whispered to him, "You know we L--- you more than life?" The next thing I remember, I am in handcuffs in the back of a police car, being read my rights, covered in my tears and my best friend's clotting crusting blood.

When they sentenced me, the judge asked me if I was sorry for killing Zach and I said, "No, I'd never apologize for taking that man's life." The Judge asked if I felt remorse for what I had done, all that followed was silence and tears.

My heart is still broken for Joe, because he lost Sam and his wife, because they locked me up here for avenging the death of our best friend. My heart and mind hurt for our families because I've caused them all this pain, without thought of myself. I can't imagine what Sam's family feels because I know how deep my own pain is for the loss of my dear friend.

Entry 58

Back to the story of the divorce papers... I know the sequence of this is a mess but again there is no sense of time in my life anymore and all of the medication they dope me up with makes my mind feel like it is full of dust bunnies and dog hair tumbleweeds. God, I never thought I'd miss the dog hair tumbleweeds in our townhouse...

Anyway, divorce day...

That broken look from my husband was all it took after all these years to snap me back to real life for a second in the visiting room. It wasn't the burly guards rushing me, but as he muttered the word, "Please?" As the guards start to grab me and I beg them to wait, I promise to be good because they have to let me sign that piece of paper. This one little piece of paper that will crush me, because I know it is the last thing I have to live for, is all I can see. I want nothing more that to light it on fire but I know it is what Joe needed from me most at that second. In this one moment of clarity I can see he is exhausted, too, and the toll this ordeal had taken on him.

The guard holding my right arm turns loose of my wrist and holds me above the elbow allowing me to have enough leverage to pick up the simple blue pen in the tray. It's funny, that little blue Bic pen, the kind you can buy in a pack of 10 for 99 cents felt so heavy; heavy with the end of a 19 year relationship which I believed was my fault that it has come to this, but I quickly scrawled my name across the paper and slid the paper back into the tray before I was "escorted" back to this cage...

Entry 79

It was weeks since I signed. Joe came back to see me again. We talked about what happened that day; the day I ruined our lives in hopes of saving Sam, it felt like the millionth time and he explained that he still endeared me but couldn't handle this anymore. We talked about the signing of the divorce papers and how sorry I was for not wanting to actually sign them. I came to learn he couldn't handle the media, our families, our friends, our home, Sam's parents, it was just too much and his therapist had to encourage him to break away from everything for a while. He was going away for a month but he would come see me when he got back. I honestly believed I'd never see him again; I mean, why would he? I might as well be dead.

Entry 110 – Almost Christmas

I've decided not to barter anything with the inmates this year. I understand why Joe needed the divorce, I just cannot stand the loneliness of knowing we are no longer together, and he is no longer my husband. They give me all these medications for depression and psychosis. They give me pills to make me sleep and pills to make me calm, but they don't know that they are worthless because I'm dead inside... Yep, doc, you are wasting a lot of time, money, medicine, and guards on a dead woman. Just let me lie here on my cot and die, there's nothing left for me to live for anyway.

Entry

The doctors suggested that I start writing to channel my thoughts and emotions in this Journal. I think they believe it will help them understand what is going on in my head... Holy hell, Joe is a good man... good to his word, like he always was, he came back to see me when he returned from the island. The darkness under his eyes was faded; he didn't look as tired, just empty. He told me he'd found a tiny cottage near the beach, secluded from the world, spent every morning praying on the beach listening to the ocean and every evening listening to the tide. He told me he forgave me and begged me not to hate him for having to go. I envied the emptiness on his face, I envied the freedom he had to find that emptiness, and I envied the forgiveness he held but I never hated him. He sees me every weekend even though we are no longer married. I still ache to touch him, hold his hand, and be held by him but that stupid thick glass is always in the way. Seeing him when he visits me is all that keeps me from shriveling up and blowing away. Apparently the warden doesn't like that Joe visits me so often, but the doctors keep convincing him that it's good for this sociopath's mental state. HA!

Entry 201

Joe's new found peace, the chaplain's words, and the Bible they gave me has started to settle my mind. Apparently, keeping this book has helped the doctors decide I'm not a danger to anyone else; and as long as I don't have another "psychotic episode," like the one on "signing day", they aren't stuffing me with as many medications. With the clearing of the medication cobwebs and the grace of God, I almost feel like a living, breathing person again...

Entry

I am so tired of being here. At night I dream of going home and finding my family and friends laughing and talking around a hot meal. I will live out the rest of my life sentence here begging for God to forgive me and for him to take the image of Sam's last seconds out of my mind. Sam has been gone now for almost 9 years and not a day goes by that I miss him any less. I may be up for parole soon for the manslaughter that I will never regret, but the likely hood of them granting it is slim. So again I write this story in my journal with not much changing and no real differences. Joe will visit me next week as that minimal time we have diminishes. I want to be his wife as much as I did the day we wed and still cherish that he is with his new wife and that he keeps his word.

His new bride knows me and we have met, came to visit once or twice. Joe says that she understands why he comes to see me and accepts that I'm still a part of his life. (Am I really???) I am not mad or jealous that he remarried; I am happy that someone is there to comfort him and be part of his life. She is really nice and sweet, but I do not know if she will ever know the kind of bond that Joe, Sam, and I had. I miss my old life every second of every day, but sometimes things happen that we can't change and can't take back. Dear Lord, forgive me for what I did and let me see my boys again in heaven someday...

Entry

The doctors suggested that I start writing to channel my thoughts and emotions in this Journal. I refuse to date my entries now because time is irrelevant in here. The doctors say this is a manifestation of my internal guilt. There is no sunrise or sunset, just an endless monotony of fluorescent –lit, concrete walled existence. When Joe and I bickered and argued, Sam would always be there...it's extremely sad that he will never be there again; we will never hear his voice. I get to spend most of my time by myself in the few hours a week they let us out to "socialize."

I hear the blood curdling scream of a woman, and then realize that scream is me; to this day that scream never leaves. It only gets louder every time I write, engulfing me in the madness of that day. I promise to be good because they have to let me sign that piece of paper; and that day I was on my best behavior, letting Joe have what he needed, because I still admired him and my heart was broken for him. I will live out the rest of my life sentence here begging for God to forgive me and for him to take the image of Sam's last seconds out of my mind. I remember that day as though it were yesterday; the screams, the thump of Zach's lifeless body under my car, Sam's last breath, Joe's "please", that damn sentence that has taken my true freedom. I remember the last words I whispered to him, "You know we L--- you more than life?"… To be honest, I don't really remember hearing his every last moment, but I know how much he cherished us being part of his life. I have told my story a thousand times and each and every time it has been the same and no matter how much I "channel my thoughts and emotions" the story is not going to change because it is the truth. I miss Joe and Sam every day. As I am on the phone, just on the other side of this thick glass, Joe is in front of me and I tell him, "I am sorry," and that he is still the one my heart yearns for; as he responds with a blank, sad, almost pitiful, "I know, me too…"

Neanderthal: "Wow, what is this feeling I have inside of me?"

Mind Shaper: "When you start to grow, you start to feel; when you start to feel, even pain can be as beautiful as amore!"

Neanderthal: "Deep down they felt for each other, even through all of the circumstances?"

Mind Shaper: "They grew to truly admire each other even before the circumstances, and that is a feeling that never goes away."

Neanderyou

Well who else

So your parents copulated and now here you are a Modern Day Neanderthal. Whether male or female, it will hold no merit to this feeling that you may grow into, fall with, or even manipulate throughout your life to eventually produce your own spawn to keep the world moving forward. From the action of sperm to the egg we start growing, learning, and figuring things out. We have no choice in the womb, except but to accept the DNA that was given to us as we began to grow; though deep inside the belly we began to feel what it meant to be the most important thing in someone's eyes. We may only have been a black and white photo, but we began to react to our mother's moods, eating habits, and outside noises; such as music or a father figure speaking to us. With no understanding or abilities to know how to respond yet, we might have kicked or started to dream about life, even not knowing what it was.

Finally, you make it to term and today is the day that you are born. You are welcomed into this world; and then hopefully given to the lady or male who, once they see you, would do anything in the world to protect you and make sure you never feel pain. That is one of the first moments in our life that the most powerful, magically intriguing word comes into motion. Whether it is said or not it is a deep down feeling which has thousands of representations and meanings for us to interpret throughout our lives. The biggest question is where does it come from and how do we just seemingly know what it is and how it works. It could be the first drooling whimper or scream that we exhaust as newborn Neanderthals; but somewhere strange and beyond, even with today's advances in human life, we have no clear way to say where this feeling comes from.

Science has come up with theories and we have even studied the brains' activity to see what parts flash when we are happy or sad, yet the chemicals and receptors seem to have a mind of their own and have no real recipe for how or why. That recipe is different for every person, yet holds too many of the same ideals and concepts that the word and its feelings allows us as humans to have. The feelings are very much the same but portrayed differently between men and women, and are in the brains receptors firing differently to express our emotions. The brain hemispheres in both men and women allow us to have emotions but men tend to act upon feelings with some sort of physical activity while women tend to analyze, talk, or cry over the same feelings. We have learned that many of these intrinsic emotions and/or feelings stem from a place deep in the brain called the Caudate Nucleus, which is the epicenter for emotion. We have learned over time that spiked levels of Dopamine and Epinephrine can cause some euphoric responses upon our bodies; while Serotonin levels can plummet and make us zombie-like or put us into an intense depression.

As children we know the feeling, but still only have a glimpse of what the word really is. Children even experience this feeling or word in many different aspects. Ranging from abusive households, possibly never hearing the word to the other extreme of overprotective and it is stated too much, to all ways in between. The word in an abusive household could come at the cost of a backhand or punishment from the parents stating, "This will hurt me more than you", then saying those three little words with eight letters. In a caring environment, the word is more of an emotion that comes from the home and family that have an enthusiastic move towards a happier life. In some instances, as children, the word in our homes is not portrayed, it is stated but only when it is most necessary. While at times the word in some homes is said too much to the point of overprotecting; thus demonstrating some of the many varying levels used to express this emotion.

Neanderthal: "At our most mature state of being young, we understand what this word can be?"

Mind Shaper: "All young, abandoned or not, understand a deeper presence of this word, sometimes better than some adults."

Regardless, this one word that holds four letters is established within us from a very early age. It is around our very souls; as we grow we take the meaning we want it to represent, just like many before us. Our brains allow us to have different scales of the word and different strengths of emotions to each of the ways we use the word in our society. Children show that there is innocence with this word and create strong connections to items, pets, and even family members.

Neanderthal: "Items? You mean like rocks, berries, dirt?"

Mind Shaper: "No silly, more sentimental things; but I guess if those are the things you are infatuated with, then so be it."

Though some studies may say we really cannot show such emotion towards items, watching a 3 year old with a blanket or stuffed teddy bear, it is believed that they really do have a stronger connection to that item than anything else, at least until they grow out of it and learn what emotions they actually have when they start understanding life. That feeling they have may be a passionate or wanting necessity, but if that item is taken away from said child their world is ruined and they might feel the same way an older person does if they have suffered a broken heart or a loss of companionship.

With this in mind, the stages that are abundant for this word are through romantic, obsessive, and attachment; which in time, all work in tangent through various hidden feelings and emotions, whether at the forefront of the mind or hidden deep within. The stages of the L word never show as just a simple sentiment, instead the word goes through different meanings as we attribute ourselves through the stages. When we hear it, something in our brain and body takes over, almost like inept complex emotions that are not visible to others; such as gratitude, sympathy or even remorse. These complex items are present through romantic Amore.[25]

Obsessively, this word is literally taken to heart and the person that it is reciprocated upon can sometimes feel overwhelmed because they may not feel the same. Once the word gets past the weird and creepy factor, it then has a certain attachment and feeling that is an everyday necessity. This word, which holds so much meaning and emotion, still intrigues so many of the smartest minds that scan our brains to see what

---

[25]   (Fisher, Why We Love, Why We Cheat, 2006)

happens. Yet, no-one really understands the chemicals and the correct firing synopsis in the nervous system to just feel that state of happiness or confusion; what is considered a state of devotion. Just about everyone is struck by this Dopamine based experience at some point in their life; but without ever experiencing the feeling of rejection or depression, no-one really understands what pure sentiment this word can hold. Those that tend to fall and never give up on the work that goes into the life of a relationship are more of an abnormality than what we seem to know in today's society, with so many divorces and indifferences between people. As modern day Neanderthals, we still want to give in to our primal instincts and try to avoid having this feeling or arousal, but when we find "the one" or, the one we choose to want to have our admiration, it is hard when the feeling is not mutual, then depression sets in at the same time. It is a belief that one cannot compassionately amour more than one being at a time in the same way, but you can definitely lust after more than just one. Once your heart and mind are together as one for the sole purpose of trying to be amongst another being on the most equal of levels, it is hard to fight the feelings and emotions that go along with it.

Many suggest that they are in a state of bliss and have never felt the pain and anguish of rejection; but the initial feeling of lust or admiration toward the other ensues and life starts to settle. Some people become comfortable, yet unhappy, as they learn to just deal with each other, sometimes for years even through marriage, as they go through the motions of what society has stated to be the normal. As time passes for these people in today's society the idea of separation and divorce becomes the easiest because mates who are not head over heels for their partner or are no longer attracted to each other, and choose to break that bond. With separations bring new puppy crushes and new crazy romantic happenings that slowly fade away after one has been with someone long enough, still causing the emotional roller coaster ride and the questions of how real this emotion really is; and if they made the right decision.

The thought of this word being anything more than a possible ordinary intuition is one intrinsic idea. We come across many people in this world; whether we meet them or just rooognize a face all while we search for this one entity of a feeling that may be nothing more than something that accidently happens. Everyone looks like the twelve people we know, finding similarities or differences to them, in hopes that this emotion and four letter word fires through the brain; and sometimes the heart will allow us to just use that simple reflex to find our true mate. We hope our admiration towards the one we believe to be the true one will be nothing more than our own reflex within the unconscious when we tell someone that we adore them. That's what it should feel like when it is a true feeling, a reflex that we cannot control.

The challenge of actually giving yourself one-hundred percent away to another is what this reflex we yearn for is; unfortunately this reflex is the ultimate and most unselfish thing you can do for another person to prove the strength within this crazy emotion. Hence, this is why some people have children, even though they probably should not. As people grow, there are tendencies that propel each other towards the feelings and emotions that come along with the word. Those that accept them tend to have better relationships even if the amorous side dissipates. The other terrifying problem is that sometimes the mixed messages that come from two beings stating this word get contrived among all the bad that is within their lives. The excitement ends, and it is no longer a new thing; just something among two people who have to say it because they are together, still trying to make the meaning hold or to keep the bond as strong as when that word was first muttered.

Neanderthal: "So we understand it when we are young, we manipulate it as we grow, and we chance to lose it every time we open ourselves?"

Mind Shaper: "Yeah pretty much, and we still never truly understand it or accept it for what it is, because we always want more out of what it is."

Knowing how we, the males in today's society, tend to say the word first, we also forget that time can sometimes be wasted, while people are learning to fall in and out of complete endearment for each other. If two beings do fall out of an amorous relationship with each other, it is hard to regain that spark that brought them together in the first place.

So take a step back in your own life for a bit. Look at the real reason(s) you may or may not be smitten for someone. Did you finally realize the person you are was not challenging life and learning new ways to feel and admire another person? Have you wasted so many breaths saying this simple and exhausting word that the meaning to you has forever more changed to a point that you are not even sure what that word means any longer? Has it become so vomitus in your own life that you only use it for everything but what it should represent in the emotional state of another's heart? Maybe just the opposite and you know that it is a necessity for life to thrive, and you endear everything about what it embodies. This Neanderthal wants to know, if when you said those eight letters combined into the phrase everyone knows today, did you grow into it and really mean it; or was it just a misshapen conformity only stated because you didn't have anything more powerful to say?

You have been through many things--- some good, some bad; but someone else has also been through the same struggles. We all grow, learn, evolve, get broken down, move back to go forward and try again when we go through relationships. We have gotten used to being let down, then building ourselves back up. Few tend to make attraction last a long time; it is not something you can make, but it is something to work toward. If the emotion ends it is okay to move on, just remember each person deals with pain and rejection in their own way, and within their own time; so what may seem simple to one, will be utter heartbreak to another, and you will find a missing piece to your puzzle that used to fit perfectly together. The world is full of pieces sometimes not full ones, some are backwards, some do not fit at all, and sometimes pieces will leave shavings behind that fit partially; all happen for a reason in our paths to finding out our amore.

Neanderletter

A chance of hope

Dearest?

Hello. I am not sure how to do this, but somewhere, sometime down the line, a connection for reasons that are beyond me and my being are hopeful. This letter to you is my expression of what I think and wish could be. Days, weeks, years, and even the simplest of opportunities have surpassed, but the inebriated feeling of being there and learning is but a mere dream. As the moons align and the ground opens up, there may be nothing more than that of a frozen chill over both of our bodies; but alas, the understanding will not be dismissed, just a long overdue saddened embrace. From time to time the thought of why and who cross my mind, as does the imagination of what life would be like if it had led us through different paths. Neither book, nor person can explain the entitlement, even though Freud has a grasp on what is felt; but the language does not translate into the natural emotional failure we have superseded between ourselves.

Coming upon the forth decade I know that I should have done this sooner. If you are still confused, then here is as much helpful information as possible. Two beings engulfed in each other for a couple years decided that a lack of protection was fine. After a heavy drunken and drug induced time, (at least that is what I have heard) and nine months later, I appeared to be the biggest mistake of your life. The question is still cloudy as to whether you were even there to see me delivered or not. The stories of you from others frighten, excite and encourage me to be better than I believe you to ever have been. Do I hate you for your choices and decisions? *No,* because over time I grew and became knowledgeable of what it was like to care for someone, even if I was not directly in their life. I understand what it means to seclude yourself from others; but to never call or make an effort, well that's just cowardly. Thank you for making me so strong.

You only missed out on sporting events, school functions, teaching me things, finding a higher belief in something, life experiences, and how much I have strived and accomplished to become, better with or without you. Yet, I know when I was younger we embraced once, when I first met you before my teenage years; and that feeling still swept over me, and I thought there might have been a chance for us, but I did not know how to fix it then. These days, I hear others say some things to their kin or endeared ones and wonder what it would have sounded like if it actually came out of your mouth. Would it have been serious, joking, or just said because you felt you had no other option? Well, I don't think you have to waste it; and maybe that is what you wanted to teach me in the long run; without knowing it. You just had no clue.

I spend most of my time proving that I am stronger than you ever were, by being normal and not distraught by the fact that I never seemed to exist to you. Deep down it is an internal battle that others can't wrap their minds around, so they state the feeling, say it loud and proud; but it is not the same as hearing it from what society considers to being my own kin and blood. I have had many figures that have replaced you, some good, some bad, friends and others, but I have only felt that connection with one other and they still were not you. In fact my friends are more blood than I ever knew you to be.

Pride would be able to engulf you, knowing that not one has been able to achieve what you could have had; if you even had put forth an effort when we had so many other instances and chances. Given that life has been unfair and put obstacles in our way, I still do not resent you. I wish that we could have talks and some questions about each other answered, figuring out what makes the world turn and create a bond from a new beginning. Starting late is better than not starting at all; and now that I am older, there is no fear or disappointment in what we have lost, only a pathway to what is to become. We both could take this chance and grow from it, creating a friendship and maybe even a continuous relationship which can lead to the embraces of a simple gesture of family.

Who are you really to me? What exactly made you so disinterested in being there to watch me grow? The biggest problem I face as I write you this letter is the way to address it; considering I have a name, a resemblance, a face, and even an ideal, but no real inspiration to actually figure that out. I hear about you from dear ones but I still do not understand the dynamics. I may take the chance to call you by your name, but is that the right way; or am I supposed to relate to you as "Mr.," "sir," "hey you," "so you're my sperm donor," or "deadbeat," I guess those would be the vilest of ways to incorporate who you are to me, but how do I know if even saying "father," "dad," "pops," or even "old man," would be appropriate?

I guess that would not matter at all if I knew deep down, somewhere, you muttered to yourself (or suffered through your own conscience), "that's my boy", "son", "good job kid", or even "you little shit" because then I could feel the comfort and realization that you cared. I don't need you to shed a tear, nor give me a kidney, hell I don't even need blood or any monetary supplements. I just want to hear your voice and the depth of sorrow, or lack thereof, when we converse and tell stories of when we were young. You were like me once, too, and had dreams and ambitions, I bet the stories we could share would probably bring us closer than the cutting of the umbilical cord in my natural birth.

I have heard that day was very trying for you, so much that you did not even want to actually have a part in giving me my name. Though as I got older, I believed that if I changed my last name to what should have been my birth right, and the name of the man who created me, things would change; but I chose not to because the name I ended with created my path and who I had become, even if it was an adopted name to match some other family's crest. Still, I know you had a reason; you were scared to actually make that much of a commitment, afraid to be what you had no want to be, and that's a father. Giving up was easy, walking away made it possible; but now do you even wonder what it could have been like to have a companionship that would never turn its back on you, even in your darkest hours, or if you felt lost and confused?

The feeling of never knowing or understanding yourself is the most powerful thing that you accidentally taught me. Learning that no matter what happens, I am a stronger being from striving to know more, and gain some aspect of knowledge that supersedes oneself from within. I, like many people, keep such emotions, which sometimes feel like a weakness deep inside that yearns to be let out; such as rage, heartbreak, or even more of an inspiration. The immortal goal of admiration to myself is nothing more than a way to prove to you that I will be there for me, and others if need be, and I will be the best at it. As I wonder why you decided to be a hushed whisper or the lone wolf, I have morphed into the leader of my own pack, and maybe one day I will be able to share my life with a family of my own.

Let it be heaven, hell, or some random place in the galaxy, we will meet again; and that embrace may be nothing more than a clasp of the hands or a deep stare into each others' eyes. The promise and chance of this may fall to circumstances, but let this letter be the beginning. If by some reason our worlds never collide again, I want you to know that I do have a feeling in my heart that is strong, and represents what you were scared to say, show, and feel. That very intuition resides deep inside, and I, too, will be afraid and scared. Lastly, the day I make my own mistake (let it be known whether accidental or not), that being will not know this pain, nor will they suffer the lack of knowing who I am. They will feel and embrace that all encompassing magical intense emotion; the strength of what compassion is as that four letter word.

Neanderthal: "I feel sad for this person"

Mind Shaper: "you should it is natural to want to have that word as part of your world"

Neanderthal: That's a bunch of things to take in, and they all relate to this one crazy word

Mind Shaper: Yes! I hope this has helped in your path.

Neanderthal: Uug.

Neanderfin

Well ugnki grunt grunt ha grrrr nnnna bbb pst chuhan, or in other words, our Modern Day Neanderthal still feels very confused about what this word is, but now understands it has so many elements within everyday life. Thank you for taking the time to read these thoughts between the pages. Until now, there has been every way possible to mention that word, and most likely a few that may have been left out. This Neanderthalic writer believes it is a very powerful word that's overused and abused in such a way that the true meaning gets lost. The sad part is, that this one word with all of its greatness and confusion, is a necessity to life itself. Everyone needs to hear it and/or feel it on a regular basis, not just from time to time. Many whom have been broken, choose to be cautious about how the word is interpreted as well as given toward others; but many people say it to everyone because they really do just enjoy life and everyone in it. Somewhere in between the two extremes, are the people who use it so frequently for anything for no other reason to put it into their language; that it seems the word gets so much abuse to a point where it no longer holds a beautiful meaning.

I consider myself the Modern Day Neanderthal, but in today's society, people would consider me to be a mountain man or typical redneck. Those who really know me and my stern brow, understand that my growing and disposition of life is very much *Neanderthalic*. I believe that two beings become one for some time, then grow apart; but the strongest endearments find a way through experiences and life to encompass all that this emotion and word is, while they grow together for as long as they allow. When people rush to get married because they have fallen to Cupid's arrow, sometimes it goes well because then the two spend enough time together that they like each other and create that special bond. In reality, rushing into relationships or marriage never seems like a good idea, but is done because that is what is supposed to be next in everyone's mind of that belief to have a fairy tale ending. Life empowers us and we tend to accidently change to fit our surroundings and even our special others' personality; but many fall past the time of romance because they lose themselves trying to be what the other person wants, and then realize that maybe neither are really good for each other.

Then there are even those moments when we believe that we have found the one, whether through online dating, or real world encounters, and they become what we hope is our soulmate. The feelings that are exchanged between any of these circumstances are all mixed within this emotion, word, internal feeling, and correspondence between two people that may or may not last past the romantic stage. We know the excitement and the demise of giving up a little of ourselves for the acceptance of another's heart. We all tend to adapt or fail to what the other person wants in our relationship, and over time we even lose parts of who we are; then wonder and question how we came to be and how we even ended up together. Let it be fate, or attraction, but over time it is those changes that a couple needs to accept and grow with; and if that works, you may still like them for who they are or may become, and that is truly a remarkable thing.

To many, the idea of being alone is the worst thing in the world; then it becomes a need for them to have someone in their lives that they could consider being trustful and conclusive with. Their hope becomes that whomever they catch, or at least can tolerate, is contingent on being the one and true passionate being that will never change. The sad part is, everyone starts to change, either because of another person or because of our own surroundings, causing us to adapt and grow. These subtle changes may be inherent upon ourselves as we start doing more romantic things or things that we normally would not do;

but others may see the changes of a person who goes from being adventurous to becoming homely and boring. This one word, with such turmoil, causes men to sometimes act dumber or nervous to an attractive woman, and it causes a woman to start becoming crazy due to the chemicals in the brain. It is weird that we forget to just be ourselves no matter what.

We tend to fall for people when we least expect it, or when it seems to be a necessity to find something within us that is missing. The problem is, we forget that before we met our partner, we were in what some consider to be a normal or happy state of mind and body, being who we were, and they were happy being them. It is the *US and WE* factor that can either keep or displace those extreme feelings of passion and cause us to lose ourselves. Many people forget that we spend the majority of our youth with friends and family; so the moment we see our friends and/or family with members of the opposite sex or same sex starting the companionship of life, we get it in our heads that we need to do that as well, instead of continuing our own dreams and following our own path. This isn't saying you can't follow your own dreams when you are with someone, but then it's them as well that you have to consider, and that's when we as humans fight what the true meaning of amore really is. We have a great passion for something possibly bigger than we might be able to imagine, but we choose to subside in that endeavor when it comes to matters of the heart. We forget about what is inside of us, and we slowly change for those we may be with. If the mild changes in each other create tension or causes battles because the chemistry no longer exist, then the relationship might last out of necessity; but may not hold the same ecstatic feeling as when first flirting with each other, or meeting for drinks and having lustful feelings and beginning down the weird road of companionship.

The way we learn and grow within companionship and those impressive, sometimes aggressive, emotions that involve the heart, are inherent and make people do really stupid things. Guys tend to change for a woman because over time it just happens, women fall fast for one and forget whom they themselves were before becoming attached. Both parties adapt to each other and become so entangled that they forget what it was that made them work, when things just don't generally work out. The connection between two beings when they believe they are enamored with each other, is extremely tough to get rid of when a relationship starts turning sour. Whether it is the first expression to an individual or the chances that have been tried in many instances with lots of people; the first time that you really know is different for everyone. In some cases lies become truths so that someone's feelings don't get hurt, and both parties start arguments with each other trying to figure out what makes the other tick and explode with rage. These all become interesting ways in which we learn what this true emotion actually is, and how it is perceived by our companion to make sure they are the best for us.

I am no expert, nor do I want to be considered one, I just see the world in a different way than most. I believe that this crazy, inducing word is a magical thing, almost miracle-like, when two people fall for the shenanigans or attributes of another. This is also the darkest fear for ourselves, to allow someone to get that close if you're afraid that it won't last, because over time, deep down everyone grows apart. I do know that life is too short to waste such an emotional roller coaster on someone who won't be open to the word in all of its indifferences, but we also need to be more reserved in how it is distributed. We tend to let everyone know that we feel a certain way toward them, but just remember that the word makes people happy and they may over think what you mean when you say it. Girls hear that word differently than men do, while men show the meanings differently than women because that's how we are genetically bred.

My advice to any contrived Neanderthal is that it is a challenge, and almost the most confusing game to figure out the existence of being enamored with another. Just let it happen and don't force it, but do not be afraid to fight for what you believe may be the best thing for you. Don't get mad, because it will change over time and possibly change everything you have ever known to be true. Even if it is short lived or it encompasses your whole life, let it be nothing more than a word when it's just a word, but know the difference for when it is deep down and should be real. It will probably happen in your darkest hour, or when you least expect it to be in your face. In the same aspect, be prepared to get hurt because it makes you grow and feel things, whether good or bad; then you will know the true pain of why it is considered the craziest drug we happen to have, "without being tested for drug abuse." The word, and its meanings, could help you see yourself and realize that the only one who can be exactly what you want is you. Yes, having a companion that accentuates this would be ideal, but do it for you first. Once you find your inner peace and it shines throughout the world unconditionally it gets reciprocated, and that's when I believe you will truly know the meaning and how to use this one word.

There is no time restraint, nor limit to the feeling of complete admiration towards another. There is no way to force it, or even change its original state. It is the essence of what is real, and the epitome of people to show not only a weakness, but the most important strength we have. The emotional bond that this imperfect word creates, is perfect in itself. We live it, breathe it, share it, abuse it, give it, and even take it. Sometimes, it is just a word, but more often than not, one of its many emotional feelings or definitions is a complete tie to someone, something, or even ourselves. It is one thing that holds stories which die with star-crossed persons; and is also the eternally, most beautiful thing when lived upon two mates who combined their lives, hearts, soul, and every shape in between. The word will have changes in its very meaning throughout the respectable use, through one person; but no two people will ever use or distribute it the same.

It is the similarities and differences in this epic word that makes it alluring for what it is, and that no other word can hold as an equal. Whether this affection that comes from the heart lasts a second, a moment, or a lifetime, it is truly meant to be a beautiful thing. It does not matter if it is black or white, straight or gay, for family or foe, mistress or fantasy; but when we say it, let's not forget that when others hear it, it can change that person's emotional world, and cause a rollercoaster of feelings.

Neanderthal: "can I say something about all of this?"

Mind Shaper: "I don't see why not"

Male Neanderthal Writer: "I was just about to explain what this word really is."

Neanderthal: "no one person or group will ever be able to do that word justice and besides this is my Journey"

Male Neanderthal Writer: wait so you speak really well?

Neanderthal: yeah I do, I just thought you would like hearing the native tongue

Male Neanderthal Writer: fine say what you want.

Neanderthal: "You two have taught me meanings, symbols, and so many explanations. It is a very confusing and intricate word. The thing that I want to share is that it represents everyone and in many forms. It is amazing, precious, and sometimes delicate but we need it; maybe not always as a word, or gesture. We want this word to come from somewhere deeply rooted and not let it sound overrated or abused; because we want our hearts to let us speak through our mouths, our mind, body, and spirit. Using this word should be an expressive way to show our emotions. No matter how anyone person chooses to use the word; it should be more than a throw away sentiment. It is the meanings that each of us takes from ourselves to represent the emotions and feelings we want to show and receive. This word that we all must learn to use differently or at least more meaningful is still the strongest sound to our ears and hearts no matter how it is used. It is distinguished from any other but all of us need it as we learn about ourselves and others in all walks of life. How it is used, stated, or even shown is up to you, but deep down everyone is encouraged to follow their own journey of love."

52 Fascinating Facts About Love. (2009, August 09). Retrieved November 19, 2009, from http://facts.randomhistory.com/2009/08/04_love.html

Al-Khalili, J., Perry, P., Wybourne, C., Moyes, J., & Baggini, J. (2012). What is love? Five theories on the greatest emotion of all | The panel. Retrieved March 23, 2016, from http://www.theguardian.com/commentisfree/2012/dec/13/what-is-love-five-theories

BBC. (n.d.). The Science of Love. Retrieved from http://www.bbc.co.uk/science/hottopics/love/

Benatar, P. (1983). Love is a battlefield [CD].

Brizendine, L. (2010, March 25). Love, Sex, and the Male Brain. Retrieved August 14, 2014, from http://www.cnn.com/2010/OPINION/03/23/brizendine.male.brain/index.html

Casey, J. B. (2015, December 9). How to Love. Retrieved from http://www.wikihow.com/Love

Cohen, E. (2007, February 15). Loving with All Your Brain. Retrieved from http://www.cnn.com/2007/HEALTH/02/14/love.science/

Cunningham, A. The History of the Heart Shape Retrieved March 23, 2016, from https://www.romancestuck.com/articles/general/history-of-heart-shape.htm

Dating Facts – Interesting Facts about Dating. Retrieved March 23, 2016, from http://www.lovepanky.com/love-couch/romantic-love/dating-facts-interesting-relationship-facts

Davis, A. Men and Emotions within Psychology at RIN. ru. Retrieved August 14, 2013, from http://psy.rin.ru/eng/article/87-101.html

Fisher, H. E. Anatomy of love: A natural history of mating, marriage, and why we stray.

Fisher, H. E. (2004). Why we love: The nature and chemistry of romantic love. New York: H. Holt.

Fisher, H. (2006, February). Why we love, why we cheat. Retrieved from https://www.ted.com/talks/helen_fisher_tells_us_why_we_love_cheat?language=en

[Recorded by Foreigner]. (1979). I Want to Know What Love Is [CD].

Fuentes, A. (2012, August 14). What Is Love? Retrieved from https://www.psychologytoday.com/blog/busting-myths-about-human-nature/201208/what-is-love

Gregor, T. (1985). Anxious pleasures: The sexual lives of an Amazonian people. Chicago: University of Chicago Press.

Hodgekiss, A. (2013, July 01). Smoking cannabis really DOES make people lazy because it affects the area of the brain responsible for motivation. Retrieved from http://www.dailymail.co.uk/health/article-2352695/Smoking-cannabis-really-DOES-make-people-lazy-affects-area-brain-responsible-motivation.html

Jong, E. (2011). Sugar in my bowl: Real women write about real sex. New York: Ecco.

Kiselica, M. S., & Englar-Carlson, M. (2010). Identifying, affirming, and building upon male strengths: The positive psychology/positive masculinity model of psychotherapy with boys and men. Psychotherapy: Theory, Research, Practice, Training, 47(3), 276-287.

Levant, R. F. (1992). Toward the reconstruction of masculinity. Journal of Family Psychology, 5(3-4), 379-402.

Love Symbols and Their Meanings. Retrieved from http://www.whats-your-sign.com/love-symbols.html

Malinak, S. A Man's Love is expressed differently from a Woman's Love. Retrieved from http://www.idealrelationships.com/articles/A Man's Love is expressed differently from a Woman's Love.pdf

[Recorded by T. McGraw & T. Lawrence]. (2008). Find Out Who Your Friends Are [CD]. Curb.

Nelson, A. (2014, April 27). Why You Stand Side-by-Side or Face-to-Face. Retrieved from https://www.psychologytoday.com/blog/he-speaks-she-speaks/201404/why-you-stand-side-side-or-face-face

Page, A. (2013, July 1). Deconstructing the male vs. female brain in a relationship. Retrieved from http://www.sheknows.com/love-and-sex/articles/1003581/the-male-and-female-brain-in-a-relationship

Paul, S. (2012, July 05). What Is Love? Retrieved from http://www.huffingtonpost.com/sheryl-paul/what-is-love_2_b_1446105.html

Popova, M. (2013, January 01). What Is Love? Famous Definitions from 400 Years of Literary History. Retrieved from http://www.brainpickings.org/index.php/2013/01/01/what-is-love/

Sama, J. (2014). 10 Signs He Has Long Term Potential. Retrieved March 23, 2016, from http://jamesmsama. com/2014/09/11/10-signs-he-has-long-term-potential/

Sapadin, L. (2013, June 15). '… But I Love Him!' So What is Love? Retrieved from http://psychcentral.com/blog/ archives/2013/06/15/but-i-love-him-so-what-is-love/

[Recorded by Soft Cell]. (1981). Tainted Love [CD].

[Recorded by The Clovers]. (1959). Love Potion No. 9 [CD]. EMI/United Artists.

Turner, T. (1993). What's love got to do with it [CD]. Virgin.

Zierman, A. (2013, August 08). For the One Who Married Young. Retrieved August 29, 2015, from http://addiezierman. com/2013/08/08/for-the-one-who-married-young/

Printed in the United States
By Bookmasters